War

At Home

Steven Cain

Cover Design: Stephanie Cain

Copyright 2/2/22

What people are saying!

Books by Steven Cain

Sunset Kings © 2020 Upon the Moment Publishing LLC

Library of Congress Control Number: 2021905234

ISBN: 978-1-7368362-0-0

The Accident in Larson © 2021 Upon the Moment Publishing, LLC

Library of Congress Control Number: 2021923613

ISBN 978-1-7368362-4-8

Cover photo: **Steven Cain**

Cover Design: **Stephanie Cain**

War at Home – Coming April 2022!   © 2022

Library of Congress Control Number: 2022904799

ISBN 978-1-7368362-8-6

More Information at

https://www.stevenacain.com/

UPON THE
MOMENT
PUBLISHING

This novel is a work of fiction. It's a historical novel. All the characters, names, organizations, and events are products of the author's imagination, and any resemblance to actual events or places or persons, living or dead, is entirely coincidental. Any references to actual people or real places are used fictitiously.

If you enjoyed this novel, please tell a friend.

To
Kathryn 'Katt' Cain,
Because she will kill me if I don't.

To
Matthew O'Neill – Bloomington, Indiana
Author of The Seasons at Walden Inn
who inspired this novel.

I wish a special thanks to the following
for their help:

Kathryn 'Katt' Cain, who helped every step of the way
Stephanie Cain for design creation and consulting
Randy Spears, novelist, who gave me great advice
Steve Doyle, publisher, who pointed me in the right direction
Stuart Boehning, for setting up Upon The Moment Publishing LLC
Grammarly.com
Wikipedia

For reviewing the novel:

Lori Lehe
Robin G. Walker

To My Readers

War at Home is a sequel to the *Sunset Kings,* published in 2021. It is a stand-alone novel. If you love this story, you will love the back story in *Sunset Kings*.

Here are some points that may help new readers and reminders, if your memory is like mine, for those who read the previous novel.

The main male character, John Hoffman, struggled with a post-World War I issue.

In the original novel, the two youngest Hoffman's had a charming and unique brother-to-brother relationship. In this novel, they don't play a big part. Likewise, Amelia had a more significant role and an interesting story about leaving Europe.

While Sunset Kings involved recovery from violence, *War at Home* is about survival and good against evil.

The first novel explores life on the beautiful Hoffman farm. Now you can explore the lives of gangsters in Chicago, Hollywood, and the Hoffman farm. It takes place within the framework of the first novel. It also views the beginning of the Hoffman farm in Indiana in the later 1800s. Both novels are historical. With that background, I hope you enjoy this sequel.

For more information on Sunset Kings, please visit my web page at https://www.stevenacain.com/

Steven Cain

Preface

The 1880s-1890s

From the 1890s, the Hoffman farmstead was the finest in Belton County. Coated in red paint, the outbuildings were seen from miles away. As impressive as the outbuildings were, the center of attention was the Hoffman home. John's father had built it in the Queen Anne style in the late 1890s. The home's turret and gables made it one of the most beautiful in Belton County. It was fitting for a large cattle farm. The porch wrapped around three sides of the house. Large columns supported the porch roof, and five dark mahogany rockers graced the deck on the west side of the house, the best vantage point to watch a sunset.

Before that, in 1883, John's grandpa, Karl Hoffman I, traveled from Europe to the United States with the intent of buying land in the Midwest. While on the train from New York City to Indianapolis, he frequently pulled out a piece of paper and read the description written on it.

"Prime farmland prices as good or better than any place in Europe. Priced at $1 per acre. Contact: Ruderman Realty in Lafayette, Indiana."

Karl carefully folded the paper as the train rocked back and forth. He curiously studied the Pennsylvania landscape, which reminded him of home in Europe and then the landscape of Ohio, which was the flattest and most open country he'd ever seen. He thought the trip would never end after taking a boat from the Port Marina, France to New York City, USA, and then the train from New York to Indianapolis and then Lafayette. When the train finally arrived, Karl exited the train station and immediately stopped in his tracks in front of the Tippecanoe County Courthouse. He never guessed he'd stand in front of one of the more French-looking buildings he'd ever seen and do so the in middle west of the United States. Scaffolding still clung to parts of the building, but he admired the two-story limestone building. Karl read much about Indiana before traveling to Lafayette. He knew that

Indiana limestone fed the ever-expanding skylines of New York City and Washington DC. He had not expected to see pastiche styles, including Second Empire, Beaux-Arts, Baroque, Rococo, Georgian, and Neo-Classical. The structure featured dozens of columns; Karl didn't take time to count them all. As he walked to the front of the building, he read a plaque located there. It bragged about the nine statues, including a 14-foot statue of Liberty atop the building. It even told of a 3,000-pound bell tuned to C-sharp. When the bell rang at 10 am, Karl took out his pocket watch and adjusted it. He mused about the fact that the town he now stood in carried the name of the French General Lafayette, who helped the Americans during the Revolutionary War.

Karl had also read about the productive land in Belton County, a few miles northwest of Lafayette, which he intended to buy. He couldn't wait to view the land, so he walked a few blocks to Ruderman Realty, where he arranged a carriage ride to the neighboring county. When he stepped off the carriage and took in the view, he couldn't believe what he saw. Miles and miles of land lay before him, divided by swampy marshes and creeks. He grabbed a handful of the silt and clay soil that he crumbled in his fingers. After walking the ground for an hour, he turned to Ruderman and said, "I'll buy 300 acres."

Within a half year, Karl sold his land near Bailleul, France, loaded breeder cattle onto a boat, and headed for New York City and then by train for Lafayette, Indiana. The entire process was expensive, and Karl lost a cow during the trip. He anticipated a cow or two dying but sold the dead cow for beef at a train station along the way. He lost money because the cow was worth much more as a breeder than beef, but he wasn't worried about the money. While he bought the Indiana land through the Land Grant sale, which Abraham Lincoln had set up, he sold his land in Europe for 50 times the price of the Indiana land.

He never regretted leaving the overcrowded area of France. He settled into Belton County and began a cattle farm that would remain in the Hoffman family for hundreds of years.

Karl never felt freer than when he began farming in Indiana. He knew he and his family were fortunate to have the opportunity, so he instilled into his grandson, John, that the Hoffmans would be helpful to anyone in need.

Chapter 1

June 1928

Karl Hoffman II helped with the chores as he and the men did every day, early in the morning. When he glanced down the lane to the road, he did a double-take. He rubbed his eyes, thinking he had seen an angel walking on the road to their farm. Karl looked again. Although she was still far away and her presence was improbable, he knew it was Lizzy Lee. She wore only a white nightgown that lightly fluttered in the breeze. It looked to Karl as if she stopped and gazed in wonderment at what she saw. She stood before Jardin Botanique, which John had built after accidentally destroying the first one in France during World War One.

To Karl, it appeared Lizzy took in the beauty of the nymph and the four satyrs standing above the garden. It looked as if she put her head back to enjoy the aroma of the roses.

In reality, she stood in shock because she had found the Hoffman farm after walking for the past four hours during the night.

She turned onto their lane and, again, into the Hoffman lives. Karl calmly walked into the barn and found the most miniature and softest horse blanket he could find. He carried it down the lane and met her without saying a word. He wrapped the blanket around her shoulders. She had been shivering and sobbing in the cool of the morning. She buried her face into Karl's muscular chest. He felt he needed to let her talk first, even though he saw her huge black eye and bruises on her arms and legs. He desperately wanted to ask her what had happened, but because it was Karl's way, he managed to keep quiet until she wanted to speak.

Slowly they walked up to the house. Once inside, Berta and Amelia dropped everything and attended to the young woman they did not know.

Lizzy pleaded, "Help me!" She raised a hand to Amelia's shoulders. Karl stood dumbfounded until Berta grabbed his arm and led him out the door.

Before he left, Karl said, "It is Lizzy. Fritz's Lizzy." Berta's eyes widened, and all the thoughts about Fritz's emotional outpouring came to her mind. Yet, she turned back into the kitchen to help the disheveled child.

Lizzy began to describe what had happened to her the night before.

When Karl returned to the barn, Fritz asked where he had been. Karl moaned and said, "You don't want to know."

Fritz let out an exasperated breath and said, "Well, now I want to know even more."

Karl stood motionless with a blank look. Fritz understood and gave him time to gather his words together. Karl contemplated what he would tell him when John walked up to the two young men. They stood in a barn with fresh straw, which partially masked the smell of cow manure.

Karl finally offered, "It's Lizzy."

"What about Lizzy?" Fritz said. "She's long gone and out of my life. W-why talk about her?"

Karl looked at the straw on the barn floor and moved his feet like a cat fluffing a sleeping spot, "Well, she's back."

Fritz gave an incredulous gasp. He didn't believe Karl. It was a reasonable belief because there was no commotion on the farm that morning. If someone drove up, Fritz didn't see or hear them. He wondered why Karl tormented him by bringing up her foul memory. "Nuh-uh," was all Fritz could muster.

Karl knew Fritz would not believe him, but he carried on anyway, "Believe me, it's true. She is badly beaten. Mom and Amelia are taking care of her now."

Fritz stared at Karl and John, then he made a sudden dash for the door, but John and Karl grabbed Fritz by the arms. Fritz didn't struggle. He stopped, shook his head, and said a weak, "Thank you. I don't know what I was thinking."

Karl added, "You don't want to go in there. The women will take care of her and talk to her." He looked at Fritz and John, "I believe those soft hearts are ready to take her under their wings."

Karl explained how he found Lizzy at the end of the lane and about her condition. Fritz shook his head, now believing Karl but upset with the turn of events. Karl had learned she walked in the early morning from Miller's Point, which all the locals knew was a hideaway for the gangsters from the Northwest Indiana arm of the Chicago Outfit.

While Lizzy spoke with Berta and Amelia, the Northwest Indiana Outfit began to wake at Miller's Point. Frank still snored in the chair where Lizzy had left him the night before. Once he snorted, and it woke him. His dry mouth kept him awake because he needed a drink of water. His bad breath distracted him until he rinsed his mouth with a used cup of water. Suddenly it hit him. He swiftly moved to the bedroom where he expected to see Lizzy, but he didn't see her. In his next thought, he suspected her of sleeping with one of the men. He opened every bedroom door and inspected for Lizzy. One man dressed while his Goomah lay naked on the bed.

Angry and suffering from a hangover, the man said, "Hey, a little privacy here!"

Frank groaned and then said, "Have you seen Lizzy?"

"Not since you waved that knife in her face last night."

He had forgotten about what he did in the night. He immediately returned to his bedroom, looked into the closet, and rifled through her clothes. He saw everything he had packed the day before except one pair of underwear and a nightgown.

Frank panicked and hustled out the door. He looked in every car, hoping she slept the night off in one of them. Again, no Lizzy. When he returned to the house, he saw her footprints in a muddy area where the men had pissed the night before. He looked around, but Lizzy left no other prints where the ground was dry.

He correctly assumed Lizzy had walked away. Jumping into his car, he drove for a few miles in every direction. Still, no Lizzy. When he returned to the house, he made sure everyone was awake. Lizzy's vanishing vexed Frank. Unfortunately for him, he had to go on with work at hand in the retreat, so he insisted that the Goomahs drive the roads further away than he had gone. They rumbled because they were hungry and hungover, but they complied.

Frank didn't know it at the time, but he would see Lizzy only one more time in his life.

Lizzy poured out what had happened to her the night before between sobs. Amelia washed Lizzy's filthy bare feet, which had walked miles in the night, and Berta gently applied ice to the black eye.

She went on to tell the women she had traveled to the Miller's Point retreat with a man named Frank Luzon. "They call him The Lizard because…, evidently, because he's sneaky. He is the man I met while working with Fritz at the Blind Pig. Others from the Outfit traveled with us to the Miller's Point retreat. We arrived about six last night."

She described that three other Goomahs helped her prepare dinner for the group of five men and themselves. Amelia looked at Lizzy in confusion. Catching her confused look, she said, "That's what they call us women loyal to our men in the Outfit. We are kind of like a second mother to our men." Lizzy continued. "After dinner, the men began to talk about recent events. The others immediately attacked Frank for the failure in Hollywood." Lizzy said, "I'll tell you more about Hollywood later."

She continued with the story. The other men were brutal to Frank because of his mistakes in Hollywood. Everyone, including Lizzy, began drinking. Soon Lizzy could see that all of the men would grow very drunk, so she faked drinking for the rest of the evening. She explained, "When Frank became drunk, he started beating her while the other men cheered him on."

"The Lizard, yeah, that's what I'll call him after last night, became belligerent. He even pulled out a knife and pointed it at me. I shrieked and backed away, but he kept coming toward me until he used the knife to tear off my dress while the other men laughed. I'm dressed in a nightgown because Frank cut the clothes off my body. As I stood in my bra and dress slip, I feared they would rape me."

Both Berta and Amelia simultaneously gasped. Berta said, "You dear thing. Take your time." She handed Lizzy a freshly brewed tea. "This may help."

Lizzy took the cup of tea thankfully and felt it warm her hands and refresh her. She said, "I was lucky the three other Goomahs started entertaining their men. They saved me from a terrible fate. I ran into a bedroom and grabbed this nightgown. I had no idea I would walk four hours in it. When I returned to the drunken men, I sat beside the outside door, not knowing what to do next, but I cowered down and hoped to draw less attention. Frank continued drinking, as did the other men and the three women."

She related, "Because of the heavy drinking, Frank passed out in a wing chair. But it wasn't until two a.m. when the last man passed out. Before he did, he leered at me. Fortunately, the drinking made it so he couldn't deliver on his desires. Completely sober, I was horrified by the way they had treated me. I mean, Frank had beat me before, but not like that. A black eye here or there and an arm bruise once in a while. He didn't do anything I couldn't cover up with clothing or a veiled hat. But last night, he blamed me for all of his troubles. I've never seen him like that before."

Lizzy continued with her story. She couldn't remember how long she had sat by the door and listened to the men snore. She filled her time by calculating her next steps.

"When Fritz and I lived together, he proudly described the farm and the hideaway location very well. I'm very good at directions, so when I mustered up the courage, I stood up and walked out the door."

Outside, Lizzy stood for a moment to become oriented with the stars and her location. Then she felt the muddy mess at her feet and remembered the men had pissed where she stood. She rubbed her feet in some soft grass as she cringed from the smelly mess. Settling down, she thought about Fritz bragging about the Hoffman farm and its location relative to the so-called "hideaway." With a bit of hope, she began walking toward the farm. In the four-hour walk, no car or vehicle passed by her, so she walked the entire way.

The story upset Berta so much that she stepped back and sat at the kitchen table with shaky hands. Lizzy didn't miss seeing her shaking.

She looked at Berta and said, "I'm so sorry, I shouldn't have come here."

Amelia patted her shoulder and said, "Don't say that. The Hoffmans will take care of you."

Gathering her strength, Berta stood up and said, "Young lady, you did right to come here. You can stay as long as you like."

In the barn, John asked, "Well, Fritz, what are you going to do now that Lizzy is back?"

Fritz continued pitching hay into the feeders and hesitated to say anything. Finally, he mustered up, "I don't know what I'm going to do, except I'm not going to talk to her."

As the family sat at dinner, Lizzy picked at her food. Lizzy's size was closer to Berta's, so Berta found a dress she could wear. Some safety pins helped the dress fit better. Berta told her they would go into Boulton the next day to buy her some clothes and materials to make more. Lizzy immediately said, "No-no, I can't go in there! They will be searching for me."

Berta nodded, "Okay, I have your measurements. I will go into town and pick some things out for you."

Lizzy protested, "I can't expect you to shop for me."

Berta let out a dry chuckle, "Sweetheart, it's the least we can do after what you've been through."

While eating dinner, the men took their cues from Berta and Amelia, who talked the most. They asked about city life, theater, and Hollywood, but they stayed away from any talk about the Chicago Outfit.

While John and Karl chimed in occasionally, Fritz sat at the opposite end of the table from Lizzy, kept quiet, and never looked at her. Fritz's non-action didn't go unnoticed by Lizzy and the rest of the family. She glanced at him from time to time but didn't say anything.

Chapter 2

1918

John Hoffman II lay in mud and blood as the squad he fought alongside inspected a holdout for the German army in the French village of Bailleul. The juxtaposition between his survival and his farm filled his mind.

During the war, John often thought about his grandfather, Karl I, leaving the German-speaking area of France and moving to America. If his grandfather had not moved, John might now have been dead due to the German invasion. After Karl Hoffman bought the land that made up the Hoffman farm, he brought his son, John I, and John's wife, Kathryn. One year after moving to America, the couple gave birth to John Junior.

Also, during the great war, John took pleasure when thinking about the farm and a sense of sadness because he left home to fight in this war. A bullet buzzed over John's head, bringing him out of his reverie. For a second, he raised his head to inspect what lay ahead of him. He saw the Jardin Botanique in the moonlight, the same Jardin he saw ten years ago with his uncle, Pere, but in a much different situation tonight.

Ten years ago, he stood where he lay now. The Jardin presented the aroma of roses. That gathering was the first and last meeting between John and his Uncle Pere.

The night filled his senses with war. John didn't peer over the short wall to the Jardin for more than a second. Unlike his peer, who was the cartographer for the group. The man was Barry Bernard, a British soldier who had the job of mapping the location of the German's hideout. The allies had pushed them back to Bailleul in their drive to push the Germans out of France. The crew John fought with scouted ahead of the Allies to precisely locate the Germans, so the ballistics division could eliminate them. Barry stuck his head up over the wall a few seconds too long to complete the mapping task. He took a German bullet through his helmet, fell, and bled on the map where he had written the coordinates. Frank **Trevelyan**, a British gentleman, gasped. Frank had taken in Barry as a best friend from Britain for the last three years during the war. They both had dodged hundreds of bullets, so Frank took one second to assimilate what happened to his friendship with Barry. Barry was dead, and that was war.

Then he barked to John, "What are the coordinates?"

John looked at Frank.

"What did he write on the map? Give me those coordinates."

John rolled Barry's body off the map and studied what he had written. Barry bled on the handwritten coordinates, which created a haunting and lifelong problem for John.

Frank shouted, "What are the coordinates?"

John took his best guess.

Minutes later, when the men retreated from Bailleul into a pasture on the way back to the allies' camp, explosions from Bailleul filled the night sky with yellow-gold light. The allies' cannons blasted the last hideout of the German soldiers in France.

When Germany surrendered on November 11, John ventured back to where the blast took place. When he walked around the corner of a half-standing building, he saw what he had visited only two times in his life, the Jardin Botanique. The first time was with his Uncle Pere, where John took in the view of statues of the ten-foot-tall nymph, four lesser satyrs, and roses that smelled like heaven. On his return visit, he fell to his knees when he saw the ashes of Jardin, which his uncle had cared for and loved. In attempting to read the coordinates that Barry bled on, John had incorrectly told Frank coordinates considerably more expansive than the building the Germans hid in that fateful night. The blast included the Jardin, which would affect John for life.

Chapter 3

1918-1922

John walked through a pasture that he vaguely remembered from the war. 'How did I get back here?' he asked himself. The pastured smelled full, rich, and tangy, like the one on his farm. 'Am I on my farm?" Dazed and confused, he trod across the pasture he had walked through after the bombing of Bailleul. That town lit up from the allied bombs, but the colors weren't the same as he remembered; they were red and orange instead of yellow-gold. Suddenly, Berta, Amelia, and

Lizzy stepped out of the wooded area across the pasture. Behind the three women, three German soldiers pointed pistols at their heads.

He wondered how that could happen. He cocked his head as he looked at the six people standing before him, three women and three soldiers with pistols.

Slowly and steadily, he raised his pistol and shot the three German soldiers in the head. The women ran free toward him but disappeared into thin air.

At that moment, John woke up from his dream and sat in bed breathing hard. Berta woke up and rubbed his muscular arm, and asked, "What's wrong, dear?"

After returning from the "war to end all wars," John struggled. He found respite in Moonshine. Unfortunately, Berta did not find John's solution to his problem acceptable. John was never mean; mostly, he moved around the house and farm incapacitated. The couple struggled for a few years until they divorced in 1921 because Berta threatened divorce if John didn't give up the moonshine.

In 1922, John's British buddy from the war, Frank Trevelyan, visited the Hoffman farm. Frank met Berta, and they both began an amicable relationship. Frank also found the couple divorced and John living in the farm tenant house with the older boys, Karl and Fritz. Despite being divorced, John and Berta maintained a civil relationship.

During Frank's visit, he dug into John's depression and found the reason for John's struggle with the war.

While Frank, John, and his two boys sat in the tenant's house, they drank moonshine until late in the night. Frank told the boys the entire story of their efforts in Bailleul and in doing so, unknowingly helped John understand his ill feelings about the war. John experienced a stirring, a change. He couldn't tell his family about Bailleul, but Frank could. Everything John had kept bottled up inside spilled out through Frank of all people. The blunt Englishman simply speaking his mind helped John unravel all the misery he had been hiding.

Frank described the Jardin as they had seen it under the German flares. He told them about Barry, who took the fatal shot to the head. As Frank told of the danger the men had faced, Karl and Fritz occasionally looked at their dad with their eyes wide, as if to say, 'Why haven't you told us this story?'

Frank continued, "After the war was over, many of us drank and partied in Paris. Not your dad. He went back to Bailleul to see if the garden was still there," Frank said.

"Was it?" Karl clung to Frank's words like stink on cow manure.

"I'm afraid your dad's coordinates were too wide an area. Not only did he send about forty Jerrys to hell, but he also wiped out the Jardin Botanique his ancestors had loved and cared for all those years."

John mumbled, "The Jardin was a couple of centuries-old, and... and I, I had it blasted off the planet. I can never forgive myself. My great uncle must be rolling in his grave."

Frank gave John a stern look. "The Jardin? The Jardin? After all, we've been through, you torture yourself because of the Jardin? Hell, you've got land, money, and green thumbs. Rebuild it yourself."

Suddenly, John froze in place. Frank's simple suggestion had never crossed his mind. The advice changed John like a desert sojourn might change a world traveler. He looked at his drink as if it were a knife at his throat. He set it down and considered Frank's words.

Having been solely responsible for destroying the original Jardin Botanique in France, John realized he must replace it. Over the next few weeks, neighbors passed by the Hoffman farm and saw him tearing up the lush green pasture; they thought John had lost his mind. John tore up a small patch of pasture along the lane between the house and the road. As Berta watched him from the turret window, she wondered if John had gone crazy. He told her he would rebuild the garden he had destroyed. As she watched him draw papers on the Jardin and build it, she was amazed he saw in his mind what he had seen when he visited his uncle.

While John stayed busy with the Jardin, the boys cared for the cattle and the farm. One Saturday, Fritz read in the newspaper that a famous cattleman from Wyoming would tour the Coliseum and other buildings at the Indiana State Fairgrounds. The Fair board sponsored him as they sought advice on how to upgrade the facilities. Fritz wanted to meet the cattleman, so he used his connections to arrange an appointment. As he drove to the Indiana capital, he couldn't believe he would finally meet one of the most famous cattlemen in the entire U.S. That trip would change the Hoffman family forever because the meeting with the cattleman became a side story to the weekend trip. After the meeting, Fritz chose to catch dinner. Fritz picked the diner where he ate because of its proximity to the fairgrounds and its friendly nature to farmers who visited the Indy.

In the diner, Fritz saw someone who made him forget about the visit with the cattleman.

The waitress stunned Fritz. He fumbled the menu when Lizzy Lee handed it to him. Fritz's mouth hung open as he peered into Lizzy's eyes. Although dressed almost peasant style in her waitress dress and apron, Fritz saw the most beautiful young woman he had ever seen.

Accustomed to men gazing at her, Lizzy found Fritz's awkward flirtation refreshing.

"You are actually looking into my eyes," she said.

"W-why wouldn't I," Fritz stuttered. "They are beautiful."

Lizzy didn't blush but prepared to take his order. With a kind smile, she said, "Well, most men look other places if you know what I mean."

Fritz straightened his hat and said, "How rude of them!"

"I don't worry about them," she looked back into the kitchen and then turned back to Fritz. "So, what will it be, my callow and handsome stranger?"

Fritz didn't mind being called callow, it impressed him, and he thought, 'She must have a good vocabulary.' Regaining some emotional control, he said, "I'll have the meatloaf with a side of green beans. Do you have moonshine?"

"No, but I know a place where we can drink if you will be in town long?"

"I'm staying overnight to celebrate a weekend off the farm. Oh, I shouldn't have let you in on my secret."

Lizzy smiled and waved a hand in front of Fritz and said, "Look around you. Almost everyone here is a farmer who has business at the State Fairgrounds. She moved closer to Fritz and bent down to write the name of a speakeasy called the Blind Pig. "Do you think you can join me there at eight p.m.?

While Fritz thought it was a late hour for a young woman to be galavanting about, he answered quickly, "You bet I can." Fritz's smile couldn't have been any wider.

Lizzy wrote down Fritz's order, turned, and sauntered, with an exaggerated wiggle, back to the kitchen. Fritz couldn't believe his luck meeting a woman like Lizzy. Even more, he couldn't believe she wanted to have a drink with him.

He shook his head in disbelief and nervously rubbed his chin.

Before prohibition, most women enjoyed only a small amount of sweet wine if they drank at all. By 1923, adventurous women snuck into speakeasies and imbibed gins, rums, and whiskies, as well as wine. Lizzy epitomized those women. She regaled about the new names of cocktails and concoctions such as Devil's Candy and Bathtub Gin.

The couple met outside the Blind Pig, located in the basement of a café on Washington Street. People noticed the pair immediately as they ventured into the Blind Pig for the first time as a couple. Fritz lost his nervousness around Lizzy with a bit of moonshine in him, but not his politeness.

They sat at the bar and immediately struck up a conversation with the owner, Brad Owens, who already knew Lizzy because she frequented the establishment. Fritz asked for their best Moonshine.

The bartender said, "It's three dollars per drink. Are you sure you want to pay that?"

"Sure, I want the best."

Fritz's purchase pleased the bartender because it was profitable, and it pleased Lizzy because she had found out Fritz wasn't worried about money.

After talking for a while, Fritz found that Lizzy appeared to be straightforward and intelligent. Fritz lightly put a hand on Lizzy's shoulder and said, "I'm glad you are not a drama queen."

Brad wiped a glass to clean it and asked, "What's a drama queen?"

"Well, first let me tell you I have a hobby of learning new words and expressions. The Chicago City News publishes a list of new words or expressions in the U.S. Did you know we have a few hundred new words and expressions each year?"

Fritz's information intrigued Brad, but Lizzy said, "Okay, okay, what is a drama queen?" She wanted to know why Fritz said she wasn't one. She thought drama was something good, and of course, she would have loved to be a queen.

"Okay, sorry. A drama queen is someone, usually a female, given to often excessively emotional performances or reactions." He took a long swig of his drink.

Lizzy laughed and said, "Oh, you haven't seen me in bed."

Fritz almost spewed out his moonshine.

Even then, Lizzy didn't blush. Fritz turned toward her and gently put a hand on her shoulder again. He looked her over entirely for the first time. The combination of what Lizzy said, her apparel, and the moonshine overrode Fritz's shyness, "Are you extending an invitation?" He couldn't believe he spoke those words out loud.

Lizzy put the moonshine glass to her lips, took a sip, and said, "With much more of this, it will be."

Fritz immediately looked at Brad and said, "Barkeep, keep them coming."

Fritz and Lizzy helped shut the bar down but stayed amazingly in control of themselves, even with all the drinks. Both found out they each could hold their liquor.

As they approached the exit, Fritz asked, "Does the offer still stand?"

Lizzy grabbed Fritz by the hand and said, "Even more so now."

Fritz had never slept with a woman. Lizzy could tell, but his attention to her moved her. His stamina impressed her even more.

A week later, Fritz and Lizzy revisited the Blind Pig. Fritz set a jug of moonshine on the counter. Brad gave him a puzzled look as he asked, "What is this for?"

Fritz rubbed his hands together and said, "I've had your best moonshine. Now I want you to try a different moonshine. It is made in the county where I come from, and I think you will agree it is better."

"Okay, you have my curiosity," he said and grabbed a glass.

Lizzy spoke up, "I've had a sample, and it is definitely better."

Brad gave her a skeptical look. He poured the moonshine into his cup and then took a sip. Not shaking his head, he let it slide down his throat without burning. He smiled, "Oh my Gawd, I'd never have guessed there was a better moonshine, and it's made here in Indiana."

Fritz puffed out his chest and said, "It's made from the finest grain."

Brad chimed in, "Now I know you wouldn't have brought moonshine here unless you intend to sell it. How much?"

Fritz leaned across the bar and whispered into Brad's ear. A big smile came to Brad's face. The owner reached out to shake Fritz's hand and said, "I'll take a case as soon as you bring it."

Fritz pounded a fist on the bar and said, "You can have the jug for free, even though Lizzy and I will drink from it tonight. You'll have the case next weekend, as soon as I come back down to Indy." Fritz delivered on the promise for several weeks. Each time Fritz stayed with Lizzy.

Brad noticed the Blind Pig seemed brighter every time Fritz and Lizzy visited. One night, everyone, including Brad, drank and even started singing songs. Brad pulled Fritz and Lizzy aside and asked him if he wanted to be the permanent bartender. Brad looked at Lizzy standing next to Fritz and asked, "How about you becoming the main waitress?"

Fritz looked at Lizzy, who nodded affirmatively, then he said, "Holy shit, yes."

The next day, Fritz made an announcement shocking the Hoffman family. He would not forget that day for years to come. It was the day be brought the last satyr for John's Jardin back from Indianapolis. He had experienced a late night with Lizzy before the long trip hauling the statue from Indianapolis to the Hoffman home.

John, Karl, and Fritz installed the satyr into the Jardin after dark, and then Fritz put the wagon and the pickup in the barn. When he joined the rest of his family and Amelia in the kitchen, exhausted, he hesitated to raise the topic of his move to the city, but he wouldn't be able to sleep if he did not announce it. As they sat around the kitchen table, sipping coffee and nibbling on Amelia's chocolate cookies, Karl held one up and declared, "This is the best cookie I've ever had!" He suddenly froze, looked at his mom, and added, "Sorry."

She laughed and replied, "No need to apologize." She took a small bite of her cookie and said, "Amelia's is the best!" Amelia turned red and reached out to Karl. Berta thought about how close she and Karl had become. Recently they had begun sitting beside each other at the table. Tonight, they all surrounded the kitchen table with smiles and warm words about the family.

Fritz thought the levity made for a perfect time to talk about his move. "Well…" he said, then paused as everyone turned their attention to him. "I have some big news." Berta thought he would introduce a new word as he often did when they sat around the table. John wondered if he would tell them about an adventure, which caused his delay in returning from Indianapolis. Karl exclaimed, "So what's the big news from the city?"

Fritz looked at him and stammered, "T-that's exactly what I want to tell you..." He looked at the rest of the family and said, "...you all." Silence loomed over them, but Karl made a swirling motion with his hand to say, 'Get on with it.' Fritz seized the moment. "I've been offered a job in the city, and I accepted it."

Karl slammed the table, startling everyone, and exclaimed, "I knew it! You've been drooling for a city life for years."

John and Berta reacted more slowly. John finally said, "You weren't going to talk with us before you accepted?"

Fritz had his defense ready. "You know profits will be down because of the drought. If I leave, you'll have one less mouth to feed." Then he hoped he was lying when he added, "It's only temporary."

Berta chimed in, "But Indy is so far away. Where will you stay?"

Only Karl knew about Lizzy because he had met her once when the brothers traveled to Indianapolis on other business. Karl, who knew about Fritz's romance, said, "You're not going to stay with that damned whore!" The rough language and news took Amelia by surprise. She was not offended by Karl's words; she simply didn't expect them from him.

Berta looked shocked; John turned quiet as usual. With a few words, Fritz turned their world upside down. Berta finally said, "What will you do, and who is the woman to you?"

Fritz folded his hands and prepared to tell them the rest of the story. He braced himself for the outcome and then said, "I will be a bartender."

Karl smacked the table again. "At the Blind Pig?" he asked.

Fritz gestured with his right hand and answered, "Kind of appropriate for a farm boy, right?"

Karl retorted, "It's not the kind of pig they are referring to." The others looked puzzled, so he continued, "The Blind Pig refers to the police, who look the other way. Fritz will be working at an illegal speakeasy."

"Everyone looks the other way," Fritz protested. "People just want to have fun."

"Not the right crowd, Fritz," Karl responded.

Berta pursued her question, "Who is this woman?"

"She's the woman I want to marry."

Karl taunted, "You're not married now, but you certainly have slept with her," This news shocked Berta and Amelia.

Bitterly, John spoke up, "Well, when the hell will you start? The sooner, the better as far as I'm concerned." No one had expected John's response. He continued, "You've wanted off this farm from the beginning. But let me tell you one thing. When times get tough, and they will, you can drink your dammed booze and starve." John left the table, grabbed his coat, and walked outside. Berta thought about going after him but returned her attention to Fritz.

The next morning, Fritz left the farm and became THE bartender and entertainer at the speakeasy in Indianapolis. With his worldly knowledge, mostly from reading the Indianapolis Independent News and the Chicago City News, Fritz kept people entertainingly aware of the news. Fritz made news entertaining, years ahead of infotainment.

1925

Over time, Fritz and Lizzy became the center of attention at the Blind Pig. Fritz's storytelling, Lizzy's way of walking, and the Boulton County moonshine brought customers and attention from all over Indianapolis. To gather more attention and tips, Lizzy bought a short black dress. The dress hung on her narrow shoulders by two small straps. The hem fell below her hips with a very light fringe hanging to her knees which bounced back and forth as she walked from table to table.

One evening, while Fritz and Lizzy entertained at the Blind Pig, five very sharply dressed men entered the bar. Immediately people speculated about the strangers; some correctly assumed they were gangsters. No one knew they were part of the Chicago Outfit. One of the men, Frank Luzon, was the kingpin of the Northwest Indiana Outfit, which tied into Al Capone and the Chicago Outfit. From the moment Frank entered the Blind Pig, he couldn't take his eyes off of Lizzy. No one in the bar imagined Frank and the gang had heard so much about the Blind Pig. They assumed they came in only for a drink. Instead, the men came to scope the joint. The Blind Pig drew the Chicago Outfit's attention as a place where they could retail the hooch they made. Frank talked with Fritz about the business, who naively pointed out the owner. Frank pointed, so his men saw the owner.

With that accomplished, Frank returned his gaze to Lizzy. "Who's the dame?" he asked Fritz.

"That's my girl," Fritz said as he stood proud and unaware of Frank's genuine interest in her.

"She should be in Hollywood, not waiting tables in a bar in Indianapolis."

Fritz nodded and said, "You are right." Then he laughed and asked, "Do you have connections?"

"In fact, I do," he said. He gave Fritz one last glance and returned to the table where his men sat. They continued to talk among themselves. Indeed, they decided they would take over the Blind Pig.

Frank told the men, "This place is illegal, and it is obvious the law is ignoring it. It isn't even registered as a business. It's as if it doesn't exist. A change of ownership takes one bullet in the right place." Frank pointed at Brad, who happened to be looking the other way. Frank raised his thumb and pointed his index finger as if he held a pistol. He pretended to shoot the owner. "But we won't do it tonight. I believe tomorrow night is right. You guys will come back around closing time tomorrow and seal the deal."

A few minutes, Frank pinned a note, wrapped it in a twenty-dollar bill, and lightly gave it to Lizzy while he patted her behind. Seeing the denomination, Lizzy gladly accepted it and the pat.

When Frank and his gang left, Lizzy quickly read the note. Immediately, she feigned feeling ill. Fritz, who vehemently entertained at the bar, never noticed Lizzy's interaction with Frank and company. After all, her job demanded she entertain the guests. Lizzy kissed Fritz on the cheek and bid him adieu.

Once outside, Lizzy walked to a brand-new Cadillac Town Sedan. While she sashayed toward the car, the driver jumped out and opened the back door. Lizzy hopped in.

With a bright, fresh smile, she asked, "Where are we going?"

"To a little hide-away," Frank said. Two of the other men in the backseat took turns peering at Lizzy's long and shapely legs.

Lizzy thought the ride was long, but Frank kept her entertained. He told her the world awaited her with a powerful but not overly loud voice. "Baby, I can make you a Hollywood star," he told her repeatedly while groping her. Lizzy allowed Frank to carry on while sometimes offering a smile to the other men.

When they reached the 'hideaway,' the sun had not risen, but it was close. Once inside the home, Frank led her upstairs to the bedroom, and the two made love with a passion Lizzy nor Frank ever knew.

Hours after Lizzy left the Blind Pig, Fritz closed the bar. It shocked him when he returned home to find the apartment empty. Frantically, he searched fruitlessly for Lizzy or a note. Finding nothing, he sat on the bed with his back against the headboard, knees tucked under his chin, and his arms around his legs. He remained that way for hours, sometimes rocking back and forth.

After breakfast, the Caddy driver took Frank and Lizzy back to her apartment in Indianapolis. Frank and the Caddy driver waited outside the apartment as Lizzy walked in. When she entered the apartment, Fritz jumped up and nearly fell because his legs had grown numb. Lizzy smiled then said, "I want you out of my apartment." Lizzy knew her words would hurt Fritz, but because of her exhaustion and wanting to sever all ties to him completely, she spoke sternly.

Shocked, Fritz gasped. "Wh…" He couldn't even frame a question.

Lizzy moved about the apartment and gathered a few of her belongings. She freshened up and changed clothes.

Finally, Fritz sputtered, "W-w-where have you been?"

"None of your business!" Then she continued, "I will give my key to the landlord." She walked to the door with Fritz following. She turned and said, "I'm leaving for Chicago. I want you out in a week. Turn your key into the landlord. I'll collect the unused portion of the month's rent. You can keep the deposit."

"B-but, why?" Fritz asked, wincing.

"I got a better offer from someone other than a mere farm boy turned bartender," she answered. Her brutally honest words stung Fritz. Without hesitation, she turned and walked out the door. Fritz stood motionless for a few moments.

Chapter 4

Fall 1925

When Lizzy closed the door and stood outside of the apartment where she and Fritz had lived, gentle tears welled up in her eyes. Lizzy knew she had been wicked to a good man, but she also felt compelled to leave with the man she met the night before, Frank "The Lizard" Luzon. Frank stood five foot eleven with dark and perfectly groomed hair and was slightly chubby but not overweight as far as Lizzy was concerned. He had not explained why he had acquired the nickname from other gang members. Also, Lizzy didn't think he looked like a lizard. She wondered if she'd grow to regret her decision to leave with him.

She settled herself and proceeded to walk back to the Cadillac, waiting for her outside the apartment building. She thought about the night before. She spent the night, with little sleep, talking to and making love with Frank and driving in Caddy in what seemed to be forever. Frank promised her the moon and the stars.

"You wait and see," he told her. "We have contacts in Hollywood. You are going to be a big star." He promised her he would hire acting trainers when they returned to northwest Indiana and Chicago. He told her they would travel to Hollywood to audition for stage shows and silent movies when she completed the training. Recovering from her reverie of the night, she flashed a big smile when she returned to Frank and the Cadillac, where the driver stood and held her door open.

Lizzy drank in all of the excitement. Frank enthralled her with his confidence. The Cadillac was the biggest and most powerful car she had ever ridden in. Within a few blocks, Frank asked, "Did you bring it?"

Lizzy smiled and knew exactly what he wanted. She stuck out one finger and rubbed it under Frank's chin. "Yes. Why?"

He didn't hesitate, "I want you to put it on."

Lizzy's eyes widened as she looked at him and the two other men in the car, the driver and another man riding shotgun in the front seat. She smiled again and said, "I just changed out of it."

"I know, but that makes me want it even more."

"You know I don't wear any underwear under this dress."

"And more. And more."

Frank looked at the man riding shotgun, pointed forward, and told him not to look back. Lizzy shrugged and was satisfied he wasn't looking. Sitting next to Frank, she peeled off her dress, bra, and panties. She wasn't aware the driver saw her nakedness in the rear-view mirror. The driver gasped. Lizzy was clueless, but Frank saw the driver's reaction. A wry, erotic smile grew on Frank's face. Lizzy fidgeted in the car's back seat with the tiny black dress as she struggled to arrange it properly. When she finished, she looked at Frank and said, "Are you happy?" By the big grin on his face, she could tell he was. She loved being the center of attention.

Chapter 5

Fall 1925

The evening after Lizzy left, Fritz trod slowly back to the Blind Pig. Everyone asked about Lizzy, with some men more curious than others. Fritz shrugged and said, "She ran off to Chicago."

Losing Lizzy only started a lousy day for Fritz.

Well past midnight, near closing time, four of the well-dressed strangers returned to the Blind Pig. Only Fritz, Brad, and one customer remained. When the strangers walked in, two carried Tommy guns, and two carried wooden clubs. One man fired a short round into the back of the room, and the two with clubs began smashing bottles of moonshine. When Brad resisted, they bashed him in the face and dropped him to his knees.

Bloodied, and with the veins in his neck bulging, he cried out, "What's going on?" The four men stood over Brad as the last customer ran for the door. Once he exited, they shot Brad in the head. Then they turned their attention to Fritz.

One of the men spoke: "I'm in charge now." He looked Fritz over, then added calmly, "I heard you lost your lady. Chicks like her come and go." Fritz studied the stranger and tried to understand what had happened. The stranger continued, "Relax, kid. We're not here for you. In fact, we like the way you work. You can stay on under the new management." The two men with the clubs picked up Brad's body and carried it out the back door. The lead man said, "We'll take care of him. You stay and clean the mess up if you know what's good for you." He chuckled and added, "You don't want to end up like Brad, do you? We'll be back tomorrow with Chicago-style hooch."

Fritz didn't know what to think, but dutifully, he began to clean up the mess. About four a.m., he closed the outer door to the bar and walked back to the apartment to another sleepless night. At ten a.m., he grabbed his key to the apartment and stuck it in an envelope with a note to the landlord that said: "Lizzy ran off, and I'm leaving too. Keep the deposit. We are both gone." He put the envelope in an inbox, grabbed his heavy gear bag, and left.

He walked to the train station and purchased a one-way ticket to Boulton. When the train arrived at his hometown two hours later, he started the long walk home. A couple, whom he didn't know, stopped on the road and offered him a ride. He courteously declined. It took Fritz almost five hours to cover the nearly fifteen miles.

Fritz wanted the time to think, clear his head, and prepare to return home with his tail tucked between his legs. He thought about Karl mocking him and saying, "I told you so." He thought John might reject him. What would he do then?

The walk began to take its toll on Fritz; he carried his heavy bag over his shoulder. He was out of shape and had underestimated the distance. At one point, he stepped on the edge of the road and lightly sprained an ankle. He considered it a punishment he deserved.

Later in the afternoon, John sat on the porch and watched Fritz walk up the driveway. He called for Berta. When Fritz approached the house, his parents saw he was in shock. After fighting in World War 1, John recognized the look of a man who witnessed a murder. Without hesitation, he approached his son and hugged him. Then he surprised Fritz by saying, "I'm sorry for how I spoke to you the night before you left." He hugged Fritz tighter, then backed away slightly, keeping his hands on the young man's shoulders. "Come inside. You look as if you could use some coffee." John never asked Fritz what he had witnessed. He would let Fritz decide when to open up about it.

Chapter 6

Fall 1925

Although Frank ran the Northwest Indiana Outfit and owned a house in Hobart, he lived most of the time in the second house in downtown Chicago. Once in Chicago, Lizzy did indeed become Frank's center of attention, as well as of others.

On their drive to Chicago, Frank stopped in Hobart to check in with the Northwest Indiana Outfit. Today's business was all about hooch. The men were attentive to Frank but often stole glances at

Lizzy, especially because she still wore the little black dress. The men talked business while Lizzy sat quietly in the corner of the room.

Frank looked at his men, one of whom almost gawked at Lizzy in the corner, "Freddy," Frank said sternly, "I'm over here." Freddy turned to look at Frank, who continued, "I've opened a new venue in Indianapolis. It's on Washington Street." Frank pointed at the map. Lizzy could tell he pointed at the Blind Pig even from the corner of the room. She wondered how Frank could take it over, but she didn't ask. "Freddy, take two men and go to the warehouse, load the truck up, and deliver it to this location today." Freddy resisted staring at Lizzy but had a blank look on his face. Frank smacked him on the cheek. "Are you listening to me?"

Freddy said, "Take two men, warehouse, load the truck and deliver to the Blind Pig."

Unknowingly, by saying the Bling Pig aloud, Freddy aborted Frank's attempt not to say the place's name in Lizzy's presence. "Well, get on it, now!" Frank spoke sternly while perturbed with Freddy. He turned toward Lizzy and said, "Let's go to Chicago now."

In the 45-minute drive, Lizzy fretted about what happened to Fritz and the Blind Pig, but she and Frank never discussed the topic again.

On the second day in Chicago, Frank ran up the stairs of his home and greeted Lizzy with a big smile. She sat at her dressing table in the huge bedroom she and Frank shared. Frank popped his head in the door and said, "Get dressed. I'm going to take you somewhere you'll love."

Intrigued, Lizzy smiled and said, "But it's only 9:30 in the morning. I'm barely awake."

Frank still grinned and said, "Hustle it up, babe."

Lizzy sensed nothing but kindness in Frank's voice. Within minutes she freshened up and donned a dress she had brought from Indianapolis. When she stepped down the stairs, Frank waited for her at the bottom. Looking at the plain dress, Frank shook his head and said, "You will never wear that rag again." His words took Lizzy back as she stopped and put a hand to her chest.

Frank loosened a small smile as he reached out and waved for Lizzy to come to him at the bottom of the stairs. "Come with me, babe, and you will see what I mean."

The Cadillac driver dropped off Frank and Lizzy a few minutes later at a vast department store. Lizzy stared in awe at the columns in front of the building entrance. Stepping out of the car, she read the name Marshall Field and Company Building, boldly carved into the concrete above the door. In bewilderment, she looked at Frank and asked, "What are we doing here, Frank?"

He discreetly patted her behind and then took her hand and led her into the store. As much as she was in awe outside at the front of the giant building, she 'un-Lizzy-like' dropped her jaw when she stepped inside the prestigious department store. A few patrons saw Lizzy's expression and smirked. They all knew a first-timers look coming into Marshall Field's store. Lizzy gasped as she looked up at the massive domed atrium, which stood four stories tall. Below the atrium, a few hundred men and women sat at ornate tables, where they sipped tea or coffee and snacked on tartines with apricot jam and other pastries. Standing under the dome of the third largest store in the world, Lizzy thought it was lined with gold.

Suddenly a man in a black suit, white shirt, and black tie approached them. He bowed slightly toward Frank and said, "Mr. Luzon, right this way." The man walked to the back of the enormous store, followed by Frank and Lizzy. He opened a door and said, "We set up the fitting room for you and your lady. Some wonderful clothes are hanging for you to choose from."

Lizzy thought, 'A fitting room. The room is larger than my old apartment.'

Once Frank and Lizzy were alone in the mahogany-lined room, Frank took a seat next to the clothes rack. He picked up a cup of tea the man had provided for him. He gestured toward the clothes with one hand, and he looked at Lizzy, "Well, are you going to try them on?"

Nonplussed, Lizzy put one hand on her hip and waved the other around, "Right here in this room?"

Frank looked around but quickly added, "It's just you and me, dear."

Lizzy didn't even notice the second cup of tea poured for her. She looked at the clothes. She guessed there must have been $400 worth hanging on the rack, which was more than a year's worth of well-to-do clothing. Timidly, she took off the dress she was wearing, which made Frank smile. With no more hesitation, she reached for the shiniest dress. She had never imagined wearing anything like it when she lived in Indianapolis.

She loved all of the clothes and rubbed one hand over them, hanging on the rack. She also loved trying them on and spinning around for Frank to see. He encouraged her to choose whatever she wanted, which was most of the clothing. She refused one she loved only because it was too large for her. When finished, she donned her original dress. Frank picked up a gold bell with a stained-wooden handle and rang it. The man who had led them into the room re-entered within a moment. Gazing at the hanging clothes, Lizzy pointed out which ones she wanted.

Frank looked at the man and said, "Package these up and have the ladies at the jewelry counter supply some matching glitter. Have them delivered to this address." Frank handed the man a card.

As they left Marshall Fields, Lizzy wanted to pinch herself to ensure she wasn't dreaming. She waited until she and Frank were in the Caddy to plant a big kiss on his lips. Sitting back, she realized she needed a handkerchief to wipe the lipstick off of Frank's lips. She pulled a handkerchief from Frank's pocket and dabbed lightly at his lips. He didn't mind the attention. The $500 plus he spent, including the jewelry, was worth the private dressing show Lizzy had provided.

Lizzy puzzled over the money Frank had spent. She asked him, "You make that much money selling hooch?"

Frank looked out the Caddy's window and smiled slightly. "It's not only moonshine, babe."

"What is the other then?"

Frank wasn't ready to tell Lizzy everything. He certainly didn't tell her what happened at the Blind Pig when they left Indianapolis.

He watched as they passed pedestrians on the sidewalk. He pointed at them and said, "See those people out there?"

Lizzy nodded and scooted closer to Frank as she peered out of his window.

Frank continued, "There are more than three million people in the Greater Chicagoland area. Every one of those souls wants something they cannot obtain without my help. I'm in the business of making people," Frank pointed at Lizzy, "especially you, happy." He told the driver to take them to the Russian Teahouse. He looked at Lizzy, "I could use some tea. How about you?"

Lizzy put an arm around Frank and said, "Wherever you go, I'll go."

Frank thought, 'You have no idea where I'll lead you.'

Of course, they consumed more than tea. As a brunch, they chowed down on Beef Chebureki and Ukrainian Borsht. Frank explained to Lizzy the Chebureki was two beef turnovers. For dessert, they feasted on medovik, a honey cake. Frank ordered a flask of the finest vodka Lizzy ever tasted to cap it all off.

Chapter 7

Fall 1925

On the evening of the third day in Chicago, Frank and Lizzy walked down North Michigan Avenue. She and Frank decided to stroll to dinner. He pointed out the detailed design of the avenue and the buildings that hinted at a European feel. The way he talked, one might have thought it was his design, but it was more about his love of Chicago.

Frank said, "All of this outstanding architecture resulted from a woman knocking a lantern over that started a fire that almost decimated Chicago." Frank emphasized the following information as if it was unbelievable. "The ensuing fire destroyed seventeen thousand structures and miles and miles of Chicago streets. Instead of cowering in the devastation, Chicago built a beautiful city."

Lizzy enjoyed Frank's description of the Chicago Fire and the rebuilding hence.

As they walked, Frank put an arm under Lizzy's arm and said, "You see, sometimes you have to destroy something to build it back better."

Wrinkling her brow, Lizzy wasn't sure what Frank meant, but she let it go.

Lizzy wore a tabard-style dress that featured a low-cut back and thin shoulder straps covered by a luxurious fringed shawl. Frank almost couldn't wait to step into the restaurant, where he knew an excellent midwestern-style steak awaited him.

A medium-built man approached them. He smoked a fat, Cuban cigar which made his eyes look smaller on his round face under a bowler hat. The man's suit matched the hat and gave him the look of a distinguished gentleman. The cigar stretched the man's jowls, and he wore a lusty smile while enjoying the Chicago evening.

Frank leaned into Lizzy and said, "Brace yourself; you are about to meet Al Capone for the first time."

Lizzy showed a puzzled look, "Who?"

Frank quickly added, "Follow my lead and don't let him know you don't know him. He's a lady's man and thinks all women yearn for him."

When he approached Frank and Lizzy, the man pulled the cigar out of his mouth, reached his other hand out to Frank, shook his hand, and said, "Frankie, who is this beautiful creature walking arm in arm with you down the street? She's not from here, or I would have known her before now." Frank thought about Capone's use of the word 'known' in the biblical sense. He did not doubt Capone would have wooed Lizzy if he had met her first.

Even with that thought and without hesitation, Frank introduced Lizzy to Capone. "Well, you are right. She's not from around here. I found her waiting tables in a bar in Indianapolis." Lizzy ignored the diminutive way Frank introduced her, figuring she needed to adapt to his way of talking. "Al, this is Lizzy Lee, and Lizzy, this is the one and only Al Capone."

Capone released Frank's handshake and reached for Lizzy, who acted her usual flirty self with the mysterious man. Capone kissed the back of her hand but spoke to Frank, "You must take me to the Indy bar sometime."

Frank didn't hesitate and said, "Mae wouldn't be too happy with you."

Capone patted Lizzy on the hand he still held. He winked at her and said, "What Mae doesn't know won't hurt her."

The smoke from the cigar wafted around them like a lasso holding them together. Lizzy happily sniffed the aroma of the fine cigar. It reminded her of rain-soaked loamy fields and tobacco barns her father tended to when she was a child. It all helped Lizzy quickly size up Capone. While she understood men like Capone, she didn't put him down. Her keen sense of men told her it would be dangerous to demean him. She could tell Frank esteemed and feared the man at the same time.

Capone released Lizzy's hand and patted Frank on the shoulder. "Is the New York contract in good shape."

Frank didn't hesitate again and said, "Excellent shape."

"Good, good. Where are you headed off to now?"

"Rose Petals for an excellent steak and whatever she wants." Frank turned to Lizzy and said, "I'm afraid I haven't learned your preferences for fine dining."

Without hesitation, she said, "Whatever's on the menu where you are eating."

Capone raised his eyebrows and chuckled. "You know your way around men with big egos." Frank didn't appreciate the comment, but he let it go. "Well, I'd better let you two get on with it. Rose Petals is special." He slightly bowed toward Lizzy and bid adieu.

The following morning, Lizzy found herself in her first day of training to be an actress. Of course, the Chicago Outfit had ties within the acting guild in Chicago. Her training took place in the Auditorium Hotel, a hotel built around an auditorium, which seated 4,000 plus people. At the time of completion, in 1889, it was one of the largest in the U.S. The original builder's goal emphasized drawing more culture and arts to Chicago. Like the visit to Marshall Field, Lizzy became enthralled with the auditorium. Its architecture featured a Romanesque style with a cascading ceiling that shrank with each tier until it snuggly wrapped around the stage. The acoustics were unrivaled. During the following summer, Lizzy enjoyed it as one of the few places with air conditioning during the hot days. She learned it took fifteen tons of ice per day to cool the auditorium.

While the Outfit had no investments in the Auditorium Hotel, they had investments in some people working inside it. Those people involved doted over Lizzy and didn't criticize her inexperience, but it wasn't because of Lizzy's talent at first. It was because she was a Goomah for the Chicago Outfit. She listened intently to her instructors and quickly realized acting on stage was no different than acting around all men she met, except for Fritz. She surprised herself by looking back at that time in her life. It was a time when she didn't have to put on airs. The reflection passed as she returned her focus to her current lesson.

One trainer, an elderly man with white hair and a beard, didn't focus on acting lessons for Lizzy. The instant she met him, she noted his Shakespearean presence. He was one of the few training her who didn't align with the Chicago Outfit. In place of acting lessons, he challenged her way of thinking. He told her she had plenty of talent. Each day she met with him, he spent time on how she should manage herself in Hollywood.

For some reason, Lizzy found herself intrigued and challenged by the man. Once, he asked her, "Why do you want to go to Hollywood?"

Having recognized him from silent films, she challenged him back, "Why aren't you still in Hollywood?"

He chuckled and said, "I think you will make it just fine out there." The man, Paul Elman, had appeared in a dozen silent movies in his career, but he adored live theater. Although not the same as New York City, Chicago experienced great strides in theater and attracted Elman to leave Hollywood and return to Chicago. There he became an inspiration for young, would-be actors and actresses. An essential aspect of his training was to ask the question: "Why Hollywood?"

Chicago theater could not claim innocence of involvement with organized crime and gender issues, but it didn't compare to Hollywood. Elman saw the abuse of organized crime's influence in Hollywood. He saw the debauchery, especially as it related to young women with their heads in the stars but no concept of the actual situation.

In 1925, ten-thousand women moved to Hollywood, from all over the world, with dreams of becoming movie stars. Many moved to Hollywood with little means to support themselves. High numbers of these women needed saving from the evil ways men and even other women – with power in Hollywood and organized crime – would treat them. As Elman exposed a different truth about Hollywood, she kind of smirked.

She said, "I've been around men like them all of my life."

Elman raised an eyebrow and stared at Lizzy. "Sweetheart, I don't think you have." He hesitated, "Well, you have been around Luzon and Capone, but from what I hear, they dote on you. Men in Hollywood will try to eat you up and spit you out for their entertainment."

Elman tried to explain the situation better. "Some men get women hooked on booze and drugs to continue to abuse them in the studio and bed. The situation became so bad I helped start a cooperative to care for, train, and feed as many women as possible. We saw the cooperative as temporary support, and a means to train these young women to support themselves in a different trade than acting."

Elman's cooperative couldn't save all who needed help. He regretted that too many who couldn't make the cut in Hollywood often moved from the casting couch to the street or any means of support by sleeping with "johns."

"So that's why I ask if you want to go to Hollywood, where evil happens to beautiful women," Elman said. His face was so tender and one she had never seen in a man. In a few days, she learned he was devoted to saving as many young women as possible from the ways of the gilded city where the gold covering was a thin façade for the horrors beneath the surface.

Concerned, she had to ask, "So you don't think I'll make it? You think I will become one of those women?"

Elman smiled. "Just the opposite. I know you will make it. You are exactly the person people want to see on the silver screen." He then cleared his throat and added, "It also helps because you have the backing of the Chicago Outfit. They will open the right doors."

His assessment moved Lizzy to her core. He introduced her to a new world of hope and attainment in only a few meetings. But what moved her most was the goodness in him. It reminded her of Fritz. For the first time, she began to see a man could be good, even great, in ways other than with power and wealth.

She touched his face. He flinched. He reached for her hand and gently moved it away from his face. In a comforting tone, he said, "Young lady, please be very careful how you use your charms. Many will abuse them where you are going."

Elman's words changed Lizzy more than any other words a man or woman ever said to her. For Lizzy, men, an uncle included, had been about giving herself to them to survive in a world of the rich and poor. Until now, she was deficient in money and spirit. Elman set her on a new course.

When she left the Auditorium, the waves on Lake Michigan lapped at the city's shore. Between her and the Lake was the brand-new Buckingham Fountain. Lizzy had read Kate Sturges Buckingham donated $750,000 for the fountain to be built in honor of her brother,

Clarence Buckingham. As Lizzy approached the fountain, she wondered how anyone could amass such a fortunate to donate that much money. She also thought about the dire warning that Elman gave her about life in Hollywood.

She strolled around the fountain, which she knew was one of the largest in the world. She considered Elman's warnings about Hollywood and felt a tingling at his suggestion she would make it in Hollywood. She spun around once and said to herself, "I'm going to be a star."

She viewed the fountain designed to represent Lake Michigan. Four sets of seahorses represented Wisconsin, Illinois, Indiana, and Michigan, which border the lake.

When she sat on a bench, she reconsidered the evil of Hollywood. Her thoughts made her wonder if she should convince Frank to stay in Chicago where she could act at the local theaters. Then slowly, she clinched a fist, held it in front of herself, and said, "There's no turning back; I'm going to be a star!"

Chapter 8

Summer 1926

In July of 1926, Chicago temperatures soared, creating problems for people who could not tolerate heat. The high-rise skyscrapers, which provided dismal ventilation, affected thousands. Hundreds of people with diabetes, thyroid issues, asthma, and other medical complications died from heat exhaustion over the course of one week.

On the third day of the heatwave, Frank and Capone talked about business on the phone. They both wanted to see what they could do to help with the heat. After a few minutes, they agreed to send ice, which sold at a premium, to the few existing shelters in Chicago.

Not knowing Frank was on the phone with Capone, Lizzy barged into his office and begged, "Please take me down to the Chicago River!"

Frank held up a hand to quiet Lizzy, but she was so desperate to leave the overheated house she said, "We could walk down by the river and to Municipal Pier." The 3,000-foot-long Pier didn't change to Navy Pier until 1927. She continued, "The breeze off the Lake will help cool us."

Over the year, she became less-and-less afraid of Frank. She continued to complain. "It's so hot in here. If we don't go to the river and the pier, I'll go, by myself, to the Auditorium Theater where they have air conditioning."

Capone had been quiet during all of Lizzy's rant but then asked, "Do I hear Lizzy in the background wanting to walk the Chicago River?" asked Capone.

"Yes, you do."

Capone, lacking any compunction, said, "We've taken care of business. I'll have someone deliver the ice. I'll join you at the river."

Frank knew Capone held Lizzy up in esteem as a sex symbol. He thought, 'Too bad for Mae.' Frank didn't try to change Capone's attitude because one, he couldn't, and two, Capone never acted on someone else's desires.

"Well?" Capone asked.

Frank came out of his musing; he said, "Sure, meet us at the Chicago Dog Stand down at the river by one p.m. We'll grab some Chicago dogs and eat under the shade of a tree before we stroll out to Municipal Pier."

Hot dog stands popped up all over Chicago in the 1920s. Very popular in Chicago's Jewish and Italian areas, the cheap meals became more popular in the depression of the 1930s. Frank's favorite dog stand was Dog Haus, whose motto was 'Walk up hungry. Walk away greasy and satisfied."

After grabbing their hotdog sandwiches, Capone, Frank, and Lizzy sat on a bench in the shade of a huge green ash tree which provided significant shade from the sun. The trio ate their Chicago dawgs and drank Bevo, or near beer. Frank had smuggled a little moonshine in a flask. He poured some into each of their beers. Frank took a sip and said, "That's more like it." He took a lusty bite of his hotdog and smeared mustard on his lips, so Lizzy reached up and wiped it with a napkin.

Returning her gaze to the river below them, she said, "The river is so blue today."

Frank said, "It was part of the Chicago City Plan of 1906. They reversed the river, so the lake rolls into the Chicago River."

"Why would they do that?"

"It's beautiful, isn't it?"

"Yes," Lizzy said as they watched a Roosevelt University rowing team pass in the river.

"The plan was all part of the idea of improving the views in the city so tourists would visit and people would move to Chicago."

Capone chimed in. "It's working, too. Chicago is growing faster than any other city, except maybe Los Angeles, and our profits show it."

Silently, Lizzy showed her pride with her smile because she represented the group of people moving to Chicago.

Frank also wanted to explain the blue color emanated from the clay bottom and algae growth on it, especially on hot days like that day. But he figured he had pushed the limits of the conversation, so he let it drop.

Soon the trio moved toward Municipal Pier. They climbed up the steps from the river, crossed Grand Avenue, and stepped onto the pier. Hundreds of shops lined the walkway. Ten years before Capone, Frank, and Lizzy visited, the pier opened to the public. Rich with history, the pier had served as a jail for draft dodgers in 1918 during World War I. The 1909 Chicago Plan called for the pier to become public. Few people knew the plan architects desired five piers, but they settled for one after negotiations.

With a few more steps, what Lizzy looked for came into view. A smaller building hid the Ferris wheel from their sight until they walked around it. The city planners had intended for the Centennial Wheel to rival the Eifel Tower in Paris. It stood 264 feet tall, which didn't compete with the Eifel Tower's nearly 1,000 feet. Still, for Midwest visitors, the Ferris Wheel became quite an attraction. Edison's incandescent lights created an impressive view at night. Lizzy tugged on Frank's shirt sleeve and said, "Let's go. Let's go."

Soon, the three of them sat in one of the wheel's gondolas, which could seat six. Two other visitors brought the number in the gondola to five. Lizzy sat between Capone and Frank. While there was plenty of room, Capone sat close to Lizzy. She ignored him because she had experienced many men pressing against her most of her life. Frank didn't miss it but, again, said nothing. When the ride started with a jolt, Capone braced himself with a hand to Lizzy's leg. She smiled at him and gently removed his hand from her leg. She didn't protest but light-heartedly rebuked his action by saying, "Nice try, big guy."

The ride frightened and pleasantly excited Lizzy at the same time. The double impact of the rotation of the wheel and the cool air off of the lake refreshed her and gave her respite. For the first time since the heatwave swept over Chicago, she felt cool, at least for a few minutes. Oddly, she felt heavier as the Ferris wheel accelerated toward the top and lighter as it descended but didn't know why. At the apex, she saw the Chicago skyline and the Chicago River. She enjoyed the scene every time she visited the Centennial Wheel.

Chapter 9

Fall 1926

African American migration to Chicago and Northwest Indiana blessed the towns in the area with something they never imagined: two new blues styles. In the 1920s, Chicago grew large enough to develop two unique blues types for the United States. The south side blues were raucous, while the west side blues demonstrated a more fluid jazz-influenced guitar and full-blown horn section. People worldwide traveled to Chicago to experience Lake Michigan, Municipal Pier, the Chicago River, the Theater, fine dining, and especially the blues.

The blues were something Frank and Lizzy rarely missed unless Frank was on covert business into the night. Situated on Clark Street, the Blues for You bar was a favorite of the Chicago Outfit. Frank enjoyed the personal recognition, not only from the staff but from the crowd that enjoyed The Outfit's hooch at the bar. Lizzy had donned a bright gold short dress, which allowed everyone to see her long legs. She enjoyed the attention she received because of her looks, the dress she wore, and the association with a man from the Chicago Outfit. Many nights she twirled on the dance floor for Frank while he smoked a cigar and other men leered at her. She knew Frank enjoyed men lusting for her, as long as she was loyal to him. That night tested her loyalty.

The fact that she was the center of attention thrilled Lizzy, which would pale in comparison when she became the Queen of Chicago theater the following year. Dancing by herself to the jazzy blues music, Lizzy saw a man talking to Frank. The man put Frank to shame with his searing eyes and cleft chin. Frank stood barely taller than the stranger when standing, but something about how the man carried himself attracted Lizzy. While still on the dance floor, she watched them take a seat, and she became curious about what the two were saying. Another man walked onto the dance floor, approached Lizzy, and placed a hand on her hip. She pushed him away and walked up to Frank and the stranger who attracted her.

Frank turned and put out a hand on Lizzy's bottom while talking to the stranger. Frank had his way with Lizzy's body, and the stranger noticed. Frank noticed Lizzy's arms and legs were slightly moist from the heat of dancing. He enjoyed the sensation. When the men stopped talking to each other, Frank introduced them.

"Lizzy, this is John Dillinger." Frank didn't say John was infamous for robbing banks, just as he wouldn't say he himself was notorious for selling hooch, drugs, or stolen goods. "John, this is Lizzy from Indianapolis. I found her waiting tables in a speakeasy there."

Lizzy frowned at Frank for repeating it but extended a hand to John, who kissed it so much he almost licked it.

Frank, who ordered another round of drinks, didn't notice, but Lizzy felt a fire she had never felt before. She attempted to ignore it but could not. The three of them bantered until Frank excused himself to, as he said, "I gotta hit the head."

Dillinger looked Lizzy up and down, which he could not while Frank stood next to her. He said, "So I was born in Indianapolis. It's a sleepy town, and it's good we got away."

Still standing and wiggling to the blues music, Lizzy stopped and sat next to John. Immediately and without guilt, John placed a hand on Lizzy's inner thigh and moved it unabashedly until he reached under Lizzy's short dress.

"You are very forward," she said but didn't remove his hand. "I like your face," she added. Then she said, "But you had better move your hand before Frank returns, or your gray eyes will never see another woman."

John retorted, "That's not a no."

"I cannot say no to a handsome man, but I can say you will be in trouble if Frank finds you like this."

Chapter 10

Summer 1927

Training Lizzy to act went so well she became a star in the Chicago theaters. She performed and sometimes played the lead at Chicago's Auditorium Theater and other places.

One particular play, Grass to Gold, sold out with every performance because Lizzy performed flawlessly. The performance featured her as a young woman stuck on a prairie farm, drearily slopping the hogs and tending to a large garden. As the play developed, the audiences watched and listened to her recite her character's hope to achieve Hollywood someday. While her performance of plight on the farm moved the audience, Lizzy felt shallow and downtrodden because it reminded her of what Fritz had told her. Yet, because of Fritz, she performed it flawlessly.

Paul Elman attended every one of Lizzy's performances. Sometimes he was the first person to stand and applaud at the end of every act. While Elman marveled because of her stage presence and acting ability, he regretted Lizzy was bound for Hollywood as soon as Frank took her there. Elman knew Lizzy appeared to be tough, but he was afraid Hollywood would break her. He hoped he had prepared her for the onslaught of greed and dirty old men. When he watched her act in the play, especially in Grass to Gold, he felt tears of sorrow in his eyes for what might happen to her in the gilded city.

You might think the attention Lizzy received detracted attention from Frank Luzon and Al Capone. The opposite took place; it rained attention down onto both of them. At post-show parties, people often asked Frank where he found her. Frank's constant answer that he found her waitressing in a bar in Indianapolis never escaped Lizzy's attention. While she thought she had ignored it, the comment put another notch on her psyche. She didn't miss the fact that young women clung to Frank, hoping he would discover them. Innately, Lizzy noted none of them had the talent and beauty she possessed, but she grew tired of them pawing on 'her Frank.'

After a play, Paul walked up to Lizzy while some young would-be starlet wrapped her arm around Frank. Elman asked, "Bothers, you, doesn't it?"

Lizzy turned and smiled when she saw Elman. She said, "To be honest, I've grown accustomed to it."

"You shouldn't, but I will give you this; it is nothing compared to Hollywood. I know Frank, and he has been loyal to you to a fault so far. I am sure you will not find that in Hollywood."

Lizzy looked at her shoes and said, "But I want to go. I want to try." Elman had no clue what really lay ahead for Lizzy's long-long pursuit of happiness.

"I'm afraid you will find these days the best days of your life." Not knowing Lizzy's true fate wasn't the fault of Elman; no one, including Lizzy, could know her fate.

Lizzy couldn't help herself. She raised up on her tiptoes and kissed Elman on the cheek. "I know you are advising me well, but you have to understand I never take advice well. I've been a rebel. I know I'm going into a mess of testosterone, but I think I can handle it."

Frank saw her kiss Elman, but Elman was so old Frank didn't fear him as a threat. Frank didn't understand a pure heart could threaten what Frank wanted.

As Lizzy grew more independent of Frank, the tension grew between them. Occasionally, Frank disagreed with Lizzy, and Lizzy disagreed with Frank. That was never good. In arguments where both were very drunk, they argued over nothing. One, oddly enough, was about which way the toilet paper hung in the bathroom. Lizzy preferred it over the top, and Frank preferred it down the back. Neither would give up their side of the argument. Alcohol prevailed in their motivation to win the argument until Frank stopped the fight with a punch to Lizzy's eye.

She gasped and ran to the mirror. Rubbing and looking into the mirror, she shouted, "You should be damn glad I don't have a show for the next few weeks. There's no way to cover up my black eye if I stood under stage lights."

Frank snarled and walked out of their bedroom so he could sleep it off in another bedroom.

The following morning, long before the stores opened, Frank had arranged for the delivery of a dozen roses. Lizzy opened the door, with her black eye distinctly showing. The delivery man gasped, then handed her the roses. He said, "I guess these are an apology from the man who did that."

She accepted the roses and discreetly bowed to the delivery man. He turned and left, shaking his head.

Frank walked up behind her and said, "You shouldn't do that."

She said, "What?"

"Bow to a delivery man."

"He might be part of my audience one day."

She started to walk past Frank, still fuming from last night's argument and the black eye.

He grabbed her by the arm, not gently, but not in a mean way. He said, "I'm sorry."

She hesitated and then tossed her head to the side, almost in her best actress method, and said, "We will see."

She walked upstairs to the bedroom. As she did, Frank said, "Don't forget we have the Cubs game appearance today. Cover yourself up."

Lizzy gasped when she checked herself in the mirror again. She mumbled, "How am I going to cover this up?"

It was an afternoon game, as were all games because lighting didn't occur until the 1930s. Frank and Lizzy joined Al Capone in his box seats at the game. Lizzy had spent most of the prep time using theater makeup to cover her black eye. She wore a bright red dress and a matching black Gibson hat with a red lace around the knob and a thick black veil that obstructed Lizzy's vision. She had hoped to appear at the game, and no one would notice her black eye.

People in the stands, more than a few feet away, never saw the black eye. When Frank and Lizzy approached Capone's box seats, Al noticed immediately. The Chicago Outfit kingpin looked at Frank with disappointment. He also calculated the potentially bad publicity of the situation if people saw her black eye. Not only did the fans at the game know and revere Capone as the Robin Hood of Chicago, but they also adored Lizzy for her acting. Even though she donned a black eye, Capone assured himself that no one could see it a few seats away.

During the pre-game, Capone stood and raised a glass of Bevo beer to salute the fans at the game. When Capone stood, people next to him stood, cheered, and applauded, and waves of people stood and applauded, making a ripple of standing people from end-to-end of the crowd. Capone's action of holding the beer up in the air had significant meaning to the fans. It wasn't only beer Capone held up; he had spiked it with hooch, which he knew most of the men at the stadium also spiked their Bevo beer. He knew most of the men bought his illegal hooch, which they poured into their beers. The fans knew that Capone's money paid off security which allowed them to sneak the alcohol into the stadium.

Once the fans cheered Capone, he turned and pointed both hands at Frank and Lizzy. The fans mildly cheered. Then, figuring no one could see Lizzy's black eye, he reached for and held up the Chicago starlet's hand and raised it in the air. The sound of the applause resonated even louder than that for Capone alone. The man smiled because he was proud to be associated with the Chicago theater queen.

Two weeks after the Cubs game appearance, Lizzy sat by herself at the Buckingham Fountain. She had finished a rehearsal, which had tensed her body and mind because she poured so much into them. At the fountain, she relaxed and watched the seahorses spew water. She never heard the man step up behind her because of the noise of the fountain water splashing. It wasn't until he sat beside her she noticed. She gasped lightly when she looked into the grey eyes and recognized the man. She put a hand on John Dillinger's leg and scolded him. "You shouldn't sneak up on a lady like that."

He didn't hesitate, "There is no lady like you."

Lizzy lightly blushed, something she hardly ever did; she asked, "How did you know I was here?"

John said, "Bank robbers have their way with intelligence on people they really want to know about."

Surprised, Lizzy said, "So you are a bank robber, huh. That explains why you and Frank know each other."

"Well, more people know me than Frank. I am a most wanted person."

"Oh, and you are modest to boot."

John put out a hand, flipped it over a couple of times, and shrugged his shoulders. "It is what it is." He turned and looked into Lizzy's eyes. "I also know Frank is in Indiana and won't be back for a few days." He leaned away from Lizzy so he could look her up and down. "You realize you are the best candy there is."

Lizzy blushed again at the compliment.

John looked at the afternoon sky and said, "Here we are in the candy capital of the world, and you are the sweetest treat there is."

While tingling from John's words, Lizzy said, "What?"

John continued, "You don't know Chicago has become the candy capital of the world. There's Wrigley gum, Fannie May, Brach's, just to name a few," John stared at Lizzy's face and said, "But, above all, here is Lizzy Lee." After a pause, he asked, "Why don't we grab an early dinner and retreat to my hotel room?" For some reason, Dillinger's come on didn't turn off Lizzy, and she couldn't understand why. She had heard similar words from hundreds of men.

"Well, I'm a famous stage theater actress, and I can afford my own dinners," she said, and she leaned her head forward and added, "Therefore, I can avoid complicated late-night paybacks."

"You are a very talented actress. I've been to several of your plays, and it only adds to my lust for you." It was the first time Lizzy heard her acting created lust in a man. It moved her. John reached for her hand, picked it up, and said, "You must join me."

"I would like to very much, but there's Frank."

"Like Capone always says about Mae, what Frank doesn't know won't hurt him."

Lizzy could tell John had reached a state of pleading. "I didn't mention Frank because I was concerned that he would find out about us." She looked at John, "You move me, but I am dedicated to Frank, plus I don't want to see you get hurt."

Rather than becoming belligerent, John continued to look into Lizzy's eyes. "I don't know what to say. I have attempted to be with the most beautiful woman I've ever met, and another man found her first."

Lizzy slowly nodded in agreement, not because she thought she was the most beautiful woman, but because she agreed that Frank obtained her before John. Even while thinking that way, she never thought of herself as a chattel. To her, it was the way it was.

John rose from the bench, bowed, and moved his arms and hands as if to point toward Grant Park and said, "Will you at least walk with this decrepit creature in the park?"

Lizzy smiled and then said, "I would love to." She pointed at his face and said, "But no funny stuff. I have a reputation to uphold."

The two walked for a half-hour in the park and talked about 'what ifs.' When it was over, Lizzy kissed him on the cheek and said, "In another lifetime."

The two parted, never to see each other again.

Chapter 11

January 1928

After a couple of great years in Chicago theater, Frank took Lizzy to Los Angeles. Lizzy gave him a big hug when he told her they would leave for Hollywood.

"I thought this day would never come." Even as she joyfully said those words, she reflected on Elman's words of warning.

Lizzy's next lessons included geography. She had thought the trip from Indianapolis to Chicago took forever. The journey from Chicago to Los Angles by train gave her a new definition of forever.

It took three days with stops in Moline, Des Moines, Omaha, Denver, St. George, and finally Los Angles. Lizzy knew the country was big, but she never guessed about the expanse until she saw mile after rocking mile on the train. She thought she'd never walk again without checking the rocking of the floor.

The trip marked the first time Lizzy saw mountains. She thought they were in peril when they crossed the Rockies in the wintertime. In some passes, the snow piled halfway up the train on each side of the tracks. On a few passes, the snow piled up and blotted out the sun through the windows. Frank explained a special train plowed out the snow on a routine basis so the passenger train could pass.

Once they reached their destination, Lizzy ran out of the train and stood on the stable platform to obtain her sense of balance again. She mumbled to herself, "Well, where is the Hollywood I expected. She smelled the combination of smoke from the train, which had not yet cleared the station, mixed with the heavy scent of chemicals from the treated railroad ties under the train. It didn't upset her; somehow, she imaged the smell of flowers or the fragrance of the Joy Perfume Trees of the city. When they received their luggage, a limo driver Lizzy hadn't noticed before immediately grabbed the bags and led her and Frank to the limo on the other side of the train station. The two sides of the train station stood worlds apart. The other side of the station appeared and smelled like what Lizzy expected. She marveled at the sight of two beautiful trees she later would learn were the jacaranda and the evergreen pear. While the trees weren't in bloom, hundreds of flowers, such as pansies, violas, and roses, provided color and fragrances.

Frank bragged to Lizzy as the driver took them to the prestigious Hollywood Roosevelt Hotel. "I've prearranged for a suite at a prestigious hotel. I think you'll like it." The driver smirked because he figured a woman, as fine as Lizzy, would take to the Roosevelt like a swan to a lily-padded lake.

Lizzy thought Hollywood looked better than Paul Elman had described it. It was a prosperous time when Hollywood became associated with Los Angles. Partially because of Hollywood, L.A.'s population nearly doubled from 1920 to 1929, from just under 600,000 to 1.2 million, which made it a faster-growing city than Chicago.

The Hollywood movie, "Ben-Hur: A Tale of Christ," premiered at the Million Dollar Theater. Paul Elman once told Lizzy, the juxtaposition between some movie themes and the real Hollywood never ceased to amaze him. Ben-Hur fit Elman's description perfectly. On the one hand, there was friendship, love, and redemption, and on the other hand, there was betrayal, revenge, and love lost. But most importantly to Elman, there was the bloody and never-ending chariot race to dominate others.

The city was still young but attracted national and international attention, especially for young and attractive women. An exotic lover and silent film actor died the year Lizzy arrived. Hollywood mourned the loss for three days.

Even though she saw beauty and warm temperatures for January, Lizzy approached Los Angles and Hollywood with fear that soaked down into her bones. The feeling of potential failure overwhelmed her. When they checked into the Roosevelt Hotel, she wanted to vomit. Frank avoided the routine check-in and strolled up to the high-scale check-in at the hotel. The man behind the counter recognized Frank and immediately said, "We've arranged your suite." He took one look at Lizzy and asked Frank, "Who is this young movie starlet?"

Frank didn't hesitate and said, "Soon to be a starlet."

The complimentary exchange didn't settle, Lizzy. She still felt knots in her stomach and all over her body. Men scurried about with their baggage, and soon Frank and Lizzy walked into the hotel room suite. The vast, four-room suite moved her to feel an *'I can live here'* type of attitude. She watched the gentleman bring in the luggage while she struggled to overpower the urge to retch. Within seconds of the luggage carrier leaving the room, she ran to the bathroom and threw up until she thought her ribs would break. Lizzy knew throwing up came from nervousness; she knew she was not pregnant. Fortunately for her, the Roosevelt Hotel featured luxurious toilets. When she finished, she cleaned up and then strolled over to exit the room onto the balcony through the double French doors.

Los Angeles was tiny compared to Chicago. Although the hype she received from Frank and others suggested she should be in L.A., she wondered immensely if she should retreat to Chicago. She enjoyed any balcony because she could take in some fresh air. Today, she enjoyed it even more.

One thing finally settled her nerves. For the first time in her life, she felt she had left the harsh Chicago cold winter for 65 degrees in Los Angeles. On the trip from the train station, Lizzy had seen a billboard with a working thermometer shaped like a round clock and showed the temperature was 65 degrees. The billboard served the purpose of welcoming visitors to the county. The Los Angeles County commissioners paid dearly for the gigantic thermometer on a mural of rolling hills, palm trees, beaches, and a rising sun.

Even in Los Angeles, where people often saw Hollywood stars, people on the street below Lizzy looked up at the balcony and saw the beauty of the woman who could conquer Hollywood. A few naïve tourists waved at Lizzy, thinking she was already a big-time star perched on her hotel balcony so high in the air.

Frank walked up behind Lizzy on the balcony and wrapped his arms around her. She smoothed her hands over Frank's arms, which also helped soothe her inner tension. She breathed in the fresh air.

Frank asked, "Are you feeling better?"

She nodded silently.

"You took Chicago by storm; now ready yourself to take Hollywood and the world by storm."

Those words didn't ease Lizzy; instead, they added to her anxiety.

Within two days, Lizzy met with producers and directors but was unaware of how much the Chicago Outfit invested in those meetings. Still, those gatherings began to show Lizzy what caused Elman's disdain for Hollywood. She hated those men who looked at her with lust. She thought, 'They are bastards.' She had seen how men looked at her in Indianapolis and Chicago, but she was unprepared for the pure lust and greed of those who controlled Hollywood. What saved her from their lust was the Chicago Outfit's investment in Lizzy. Few men would prey on her because of the gangster's hold on her.

One day, Lizzy had an appointment with a significant producer. When she arrived for the meeting, a young woman exited and closed the producer's office door. She sheepishly looked at Lizzy while rearranging her outfit and zipped up the back of her short skirt. Hollywood led the trend of short skirts during the 1920s. Lizzy was appalled. Still, she met with the man but with less-than-ideal thoughts about him. The entire time the man talked to Lizzy, he leered at her. His staring eyes moved up and down her body, and it revolted her, especially because she knew he had just had sexual relations with a woman minutes ago. She glanced around the huge office and noticed an attached bathroom. She wondered if he took the time to clean up before she walked into the room.

After a brief conversation that took too long for Lizzy, the man gave her his card and said, "If there is anything we can do together, I will let you know and, in the meantime, if there's anything you can do for me, be sure to let me know." While he looked at her from head to toe, his cheesy smile infuriated Lizzy. She wanted to smack him in the face. She was unsure why she held off; she wrote it off to being new to the area.

She didn't know it at the time, but she would become the talk of Hollywood directors and producers. The only thing that kept most of the creeps at bay was the Chicago Outfit protecting her.

By May, she should have been ecstatic because she had made it! She had a contract as the lead in a silent movie. Production on the film started in June. Even though she should have been happy, she sometimes felt suffocated because of the clawing of lechers.

Soon after signing her contract, Frank had to fly back to Chicago. The flight took two days each way but was quicker than the train. Frank told her the business would probably take three days. He maintained

Lizzy in the suite in the Roosevelt Hotel while he attended to Chicago business.

Within a day of Frank's departure, the producer, who had sex with the young woman who sheepishly left his office, showed up at the Roosevelt Hotel. Lizzy enjoyed the warmth outside by the pool on a sun lounger. Her swimsuit amplified her breasts, and it accentuated her long legs, even with the skirt. At noon, when the temperature reached 75 degrees, she drank fresh orange juice and a bit of vodka and enjoyed her moment in the sun's warmth. She never forgot it was probably thirty degrees, cold, and windy back home in Chicago.

When the man sat beside her and clanked two glasses down on the drink table, he announced proudly, "These are shots of absinthe." Then he looked around to make sure nobody heard him talk about the banned substance.

Lizzy was stunned. She asked, "How did you know I was here?"

He lingered to answer her while he drank in her beauty. He leered at her cleavage and long legs in her bathing suit unabashedly. Finally, he said, "Everyone knows where Frank stays and brings young ladies when he comes to Hollywood. Also, I know he went back to Chicago for business." The man gave an impetuous look at Lizzy. As beautiful as Lizzy ever looked in Indianapolis with the short black dress or in Chicago with all the clothes Frank had bought her, she shined in the sunlight in the skimpy, for the time, swimsuit Frank bought her.

The producer made no small attempt to hide his sexual attraction for Lizzy. He saw her in a swimsuit, and the bulge in his pants showed it. Lizzy could see the bulge in his pants and wanted to puke.

The man said, "You are far more attractive than the last 100 women I've seen."

Lizzy thought about what he said for a moment and wanted to question his reasoning. 'So, is there's one woman out there who is more attractive than me?' She wondered if he snared her, or did the woman reject him as she would do now? Her face gave her thoughts away.

The man frowned and said, "There's no one like you." He reached for her legs and said, "Those will be the sight of Hollywood."

Lizzy made a reflex of gratitude but gently pushed his hand away.

The man blurted out, "I love you."

His words caught Lizzy entirely by surprise; she cringed. Still, she knew it was simply lusting. Her look reflected her mood toward the man.

He continued, "No, you don't understand." He leered at her inner thighs, exposed by her tiny swimsuit. "Frank only wants to use you."

The man looked at Lizzy from her face, breasts, and to her legs and said, "I want to marry you."

Lizzy, having heard proposals in many different ways, shrugged him off. The man reached over again and put a hand on her thigh. Lizzy jumped up and shouted at the man.

"You lecher! I saw the woman leave your office the other day. You should be ashamed of yourself."

"But she is not nearly as beautiful as you. You make me want to taste all of you."

Lizzy cringed for the second time and rolled her head back; her eyes glared at him with disgust. "You snake. I will never work with you." Lizzy had never defied a man that way. Inside she glowed because her harsh words showed she had changed. The encounter marked the first time Lizzy began to control her interactions with lecherous men.

Dejected, the man stood and started to leave, but he stopped, drank both shots of absinthe, and took one last leering sight of Lizzy. He pointed at her and said, "With your attitude, you are correct. You never will." He turned and slunk away.

Chapter 12

End of May 1928

Remembering what Paul Elman told her, Lizzy grew disillusioned with Hollywood because men treated women like chattel. When she had watched a silent movie, she had never dreamed of what went on behind the scenes. But slowly, she experienced more and more disgust in the gilded city.

While meeting several people at a studio, an upcoming director invited her to an afternoon after-work gathering.

"Please join us; I'll introduce you to some people you might like."

Without Frank, she hesitated but decided she could not be a wallflower in Hollywood, so she accepted. Once she entered the underground establishment, it reminded her of the Blind Pig, but much more ornate and extensive. While many beautiful women were at the gathering, the director who had invited her clung close to her. Stars and starlets mingled and partied with directors and producers. Lizzy breathed a sigh of relief when she determined the party was not a mushing party but a legitimate mingling of the elite in Hollywood.

After only a few drinks, he leaned in closer to her and asked, "Do you want to get out of here?"

Lizzy leaned back because she didn't expect those 'come on' words from this director, whom she would work with on the next movie. She frowned and said, "We just got here. Why would I want to leave?"

The director pulled a thin pouch of drugs out of his coat pocket. He shook it and said, "It doesn't look like much, but I can make it worth your while if you come with me."

Lizzy rolled her eyes and said, "That's quite enough!" She pushed him away and walked to the door. He started to pursue her, but another woman, who knew the director had some drugs, stepped in and put a hand on his coat pocket. Lizzy didn't hear what she said as she stepped outside and hailed a taxi back to the Roosevelt.

While Frank was still in Chicago on business, Lizzy decided to visit one of the women's cooperatives that Elman had established. By two p.m., she stepped out into the hot Hollywood day. The weather was stifling, but she was determined to complete her mission. Instead of calling for the chauffeur, she took a taxi. She had previously penned Elman and asked for the address. When she gave it to the driver, he questioned her. "Do you really want to go to that part of town?" he asked.

"What do you mean by that question?"

"Well, it just isn't the kind of place where someone like you should go, especially alone." The driver looked at Lizzy and drank in her beauty.

His words took Lizzy by surprise. "Well, it's not for you to decide. Are you going to take me, or must I hail another cab?"

The driver turned to the front of the cab and put the taxi into gear. "Okay, lady, it's your dimes." Because the location lay east of the Roosevelt, the driver made a U-turn and drove toward the cooperative. He followed Hollywood Boulevard.

Smiling at one intersection, Lizzy looked north and saw the Hollywood sign up in the hills above the town. She looked back at the splendor of the Roosevelt Hotel, which was only two years old. With its Spanish Colonial architecture, the twelve-story Roosevelt stood out proudly among the other buildings on the boulevard. Lizzy had walked through the arched entryway many times, but today she felt free from the Roosevelt.

She leaned back, happy to be out on her own to enjoy the city. Those feelings would change soon. Lizzy began to realize when she took the limousine; the chauffeur driver avoided the ugly part of Hollywood and L.A. After a few blocks, she saw women who could have been on the silver screen standing at street corners dressed like vaudeville actresses. Some wore outfits featuring skinny waists and thigh-high stockinged legs, which Lizzy had not seen in Indianapolis. Some women wore more skimpy clothes than her swimsuit. One woman displayed huge cleavage in front and a peplum extending down from her waist on her rear. Lizzy wasn't sure, but she thought the peplum was the only clothing covering her bottom. At one corner, three women flirted with two cops, which was an act to keep the coppers friendly. Lizzy's mood dampened quickly. She had never seen women working the streets, in the daylight, in Chicago or Indianapolis. Still, she kept her resolve to explore.

It thrilled her to arrive at the cooperative Elman started several years ago. When she looked at the cooperative, she thought of an abandoned military barracks. It was painted white with one purple door and purple shutters on every window. Lizzy figure Elman had intended to provide a festive look, but the purple on the white barracks made her think of disparity. She paid and tipped the driver well, in dollars, not dimes. She said, "There's plenty more if you'll wait for me."

The driver smiled and said, "For that amount, I can wait all day." Unbeknownst to Lizzy, the driver felt relief waiting for the young woman who didn't know the trouble she might walk into that day.

When she walked into the cooperative, a greeter welcomed her. "Are you here seeking shelter?" the woman asked. The greeter looked at how Lizzy dressed. "Of course, you're not seeking shelter. Are you looking out for someone else?" The front office of the cooperative smelled sterile and looked bleak. Simple decorations did not improve the aesthetics. The woman sat on her seat at the front desk with one fresh flower in a vase.

Unsure of what she would do next, Lizzy said, "Not today. I'm here because a friend helped start this cooperative."

Without hesitation, the greeter stood and said, "You must be speaking of Mr. Elman!"

"Yes, that's exactly whom I'm talking about."

Lizzy watched a resident woman enter. She wasn't dressed for vaudeville; instead, she wore a white blouse and simple gray rayon skirt, but she did sport high-heeled shoes. The woman hesitated and looked at Lizzy and unabashedly said. "Ma'am, you don't belong here." Instead of waiting for Lizzy's response, she walked on past.

The greeter reached out to Lizzy and whispered, "Some of the women here have seen tough times, and it hurts when they see someone like you. Don't take any offense."

Lizzy hadn't considered dressing down for the occasion. That instant, she realized she didn't have any clothes in which to dress down. She had become accustomed to dressing for Frank, whether he was there or not. Given the situation she now found herself in, she was ashamed. She slowly and softly shook her head and said, "No offense taken." When she looked at the greeter, she said, "Yes. I know Mr. Elman very well. He helped prepare me for Hollywood as best as he could."

The greeter clapped her hands and smiled. With a bit of bounce, she asked, "How is he?"

"He's doing very well. Does the woman, who just passed, work in Hollywood?"

"Oh no. She won't have anything to do with Hollywood anymore. It could be part of her attitude toward you. She can tell you are someone who has made the cut. Is she right?"

Lizzy didn't know how to answer. She blurted, "I-I guess you can say that." Then she added, "How many women live here?"

"We have 112 registered. Plus, we have a few temporaries who come and go." The greeter returned the conversation to Mr. Elman. "How did you connect with him? He is outstanding toward women."

"He was part of the training package at the Auditorium Theater in Chicago."

"Oh, yes, I forgot he went back there. Is he still acting?"

"Yes, but not as much as he used to. Age is catching up with him," Lizzy said with a fondness for Elman. Changing the subject, she asked, "Where does that woman work?"

"At a bank down the street."

"Why doesn't she go back home?"

"Well, there's a different story for every woman here. I cannot talk specifics about any woman; that's our policy. After what they've been through, I can say many cannot or will not return home because they lack the funds to do so or out of shame. Others have been discarded and have no home in which to return."

Saddened by the plight of so many women, Lizzy listened intently.

"I am sure you saw some of the ladies of the night and the junkies on your ride here from Hollywood, right?"

Lizzy had never heard the term "ladies of the night," and she had not seen a "junkie" here or in Chicago. She told the greeter she had never heard of them.

"Well, you must not have driven down any alleys. The junkies are everywhere; they are Hollywood's used and rejected women. The underground quickly sweeps them up. We try to help them, as do a few other cooperatives, but there are too many of them and too few of us. Some wouldn't seek help even if we offered it."

The information astonished Lizzy. She asked, "What can I do to help?"

"For yourself? Don't let them use you because it looks like you will make it. Help women around you, so they don't become used and discarded."

"What causes this to happen?"

"Simple. Greed and lust. You are living in Sodom and Gomorrah."

Lizzy looked down at the floor and shook her head. "You seem to know what these women experienced..."

"I am one of these women. If Paul Elman hadn't helped, I would likely be out on the street trading sex for money."

Lizzy reached out and touched the woman's hand and asked, "Is there anything I can do for you."

The woman patted Lizzy's hand. "You already have. You are a star who cares about others. I can see it in you. Maybe, if you make a lot of money, you can contribute to the cooperative as Mr. Elman does."

Lizzy nodded and said, "I hope so." She chatted with the greeter for a few minutes more while a few other plainly dressed women came and left the cooperative. They all gave Lizzy cold stares. Finally, Lizzy said she had to go. She thanked the greeter, thinking of what the woman had just said. 'You must not have driven down any alleys.'

In the taxi, she said, "Back to the Roosevelt." She sat and thought. Within a block, she exclaimed, "Go down as many alleys as you can."

The driver blew a raspberry. After a second, he said, "Sorry. I'm not sure you want to see what happens there."

"I want to see it all. I want to see the underbelly of Hollywood."

The driver shook his head and accepted that the woman was on a mission and he would be paid handsomely for her mission. He determined to show her the worst of it. With one turn near the cooperative, he drove her down one of the worst alleys in the area. The driver knew because he had delivered and waited on several Johns in the alley. Lizzy was shocked at what she saw. Only a few blocks from where women slept safely in the cooperative, she entered a hell she never expected. Again, she saw scantily clad women; some dressed only in negligees. One had her face buried in a man's lap. Two women were kissing and caressing each other. One had passed out on the alley; a John had left the woman with her skirt above her waist.

"What is this?" Lizzy protested.

"You are witnessing the Hollywood they don't tell you about on the silver screen. You don't see this unless you drive through it like we are now," the driver said. "Opium, opioids, and cocaine drive what you see now."

"Stop," Lizzy said.

"You ain't getting out here, madame."

"You just watch me." Even before he stopped the car, Lizzy opened the door. The driver obliged and stopped the taxi.

Lizzy stared and watched as a woman injected her arm with morphine or heroin; she didn't know which. Enthralled, she walked over to the woman and sat in the alley next to her. The grime of the alley marred Lizzy's fine clothing. The woman looked as if she would vomit because of her reaction to the drug. Lizzy wanted to vomit

because she had never seen such a sight. The smell in the alley was a

mixture of vomit and cum. Later, the taxi driver would tell Lizzy the

vomit was real, but the latter smell emanated from the Callery pear

tree. She reached for the woman's arm, but the woman pulled it away.

Instead, she turned and stared at Lizzy as if she was an angel. The

woman slowly reached a hand out to Lizzy and touched her face. The

gesture made Lizzy feel uncomfortable, but she allowed it.

To sit in an ally with Hollywood rejects drove Lizzy beyond

recognition of herself. An overwhelming sense of wrongness spread

across her mind and body. The dirty alley soiled her mind. She felt as if

she had become one of these women for a fleeting moment. She put

her hands on the alley road and gripped the dirty concrete. She

transformed into their world; she felt a sudden empathy to do their

drugs so she would better know what they felt. She wanted to sell

herself to any man, not for money, but to pay for her sins. One of the

more aware prostitutes shouted at Lizzy. "Get back to your penthouse,

girl. You don't belong here."

Having witnessed the heated exchange, the taxi driver climbed

out of his car and approached Lizzy.

Lizzy looked at the prostitute and said, "I want to help."

The prostitute said, "You got money?"

Lizzy opened her purse and handed her eighty dollars. The woman

grabbed the money and tucked it into her bra. "Thanks, lady. I will protect you from the assholes on this alley." Then she pointed at a pimp, who had begun to walk toward Lizzy. "You'd better get back in the cab and the hell out of here."

Suddenly, the cab driver grabbed Lizzy by the hand and pulled her up.

Looking at the pimp, Lizzy didn't hesitate. She followed the driver to the taxi, crying, and said, "Get us out of here."

He said, "I tried to tell you. Oh, and the money you gave her, that pimp will take it and buy more drugs for the women."

Lizzy paid the driver well when he pulled up to the Roosevelt. She paid him ten times what he would have made on an average day. She rushed out of the taxi and to her room. She turned on the bathwater, stripped, and hurriedly climbed into the bath. She cried for a solid hour in the tub by herself.

Chapter 13

June 1

Frank returned to the Roosevelt Hotel with great stories about his Chicago and Northwest Indiana work. Particularly, he showed pride when he talked about helping the steel industry avert a strike like the one in 1919 that resulted in riots and 4,000 US military clamping down, mainly in Gary, Indiana.

"I accomplished it without a single person hurt or a single gunshot," he told Lizzy, "The Chicago Outfit seized more control of the steel industry. The result means huge profits for Capone and myself."

The averted strike would enhance Frank's stature in the Chicago Outfit; it helped big business, it helped a few of the union workers who received cash under the table, but alas, it didn't help the ordinary worker except they kept their jobs.

Suddenly Frank stopped talking about himself and looked at Lizzy. He spread out his arms and gave her a firm and happy hug. "But I must say, it's great to see you again."

Still disturbed by what she saw in Hollywood, Lizzy couldn't muster up the happiness Frank felt. He didn't miss her reaction. He took a step back but held her shoulders. Stooping down, he looked into her eyes and asked, "What's wrong, baby? You can tell Frankie."

To avoid his eyes, Lizzy looked at the floor. She hesitated but finally said, "I'm not enjoying Hollywood."

"What?" Frank exclaimed.

Lizzy stretched one arm toward the window as if she pointed at all Hollywood. A single tear rolled down her cheek. "This place," she hesitated, "This place is horrid."

Frank shook his head, "Hollywood is your future."

Lizzy said nothing but slowly shook her head.

Frank walked over to their room bar icebox, pulled out a champagne bottle, opened it, and poured it into two glasses. He handed her one and toasted to her and said, "In a few weeks, your first major silent film begins production. You'll feel better then." He smiled, and with sharp eyes, he snapped his fingers and then pointed at her. "I know what it is! You're experiencing preproduction blues."

Lizzy had never heard of preproduction blues and did not want to tell him about the producer hitting on her, the cooperative she visited, or the junkie she sat next to in the alley.

Frank continued. "I know what you need. The studio we're working with is throwing an enormous party tomorrow night. Everyone who is anyone in Hollywood will be there."

Lizzy wanted to tell Frank what she had seen while he was gone, but she felt it best she kept quiet and sipped her champagne.

Lizzy found out the event Frank mentioned was a mushing party. She had heard of them in Chicago, where they were called petting parties. She didn't want to go, but her curiosity took the better of her, and she felt Frank would protect her. When they walked into the ballroom, the producer for her film and several of the crew drew their attention. The producer had not shown a lecherous side, but Lizzy figured it was only a matter of time.

"Frank, it's so good to see you again," the producer reached out and shook his hand. "Production is moving forward," then he winked at Frank, "Thanks to your investment." Lizzy didn't make eye contact with him, but he reached out, put a hand on Lizzy's chin, and said, "It's good to see you again, Lizzy." She didn't know why, but she figured what he said was false. A waiter arrived with a mixture of cocktails, all prohibited in the 1920s. Frank chose the neat bourbon. Lizzy started to reach for white wine, but the producer grabbed her arm. He smiled at Lizzy and said, "This is a mushing party! My dear, you want something stronger." He reached for and grabbed a gin and placed it into her hand. Frank didn't seem to mind the interruption by the producer because he busied himself scanning the room. Lizzy accepted the more potent drink but immediately pulled her other hand away from the producer. She thought, 'Now it begins.' When Frank finished studying the room, he began talking to the producer again, but not before he grabbed a second bourbon.

Lizzy wanted to separate herself from the producer, so she began to stroll around the ballroom. At first, she thought it was only the cast and crew of a few upcoming films, which included the one in which she would star. As she strolled around the room, she began to see flappers who placed their hands all over certain men. The men returned the action by erotically touching the flappers. All the women wore their hair short and wore loose-fitting slip-over dresses. It was early June in Hollywood, so all the dresses were sleeveless. One flapper stood with one leg between a man's legs as she moved it up and down to softly rub against his genitals.

Lizzy felt the public sexual display sickened her. She stepped out on the balcony, where she saw men and women caressing each other. She thought she had seen several of the women working around the studios the past few weeks, and she knew some of the men. She leaned against the concrete balcony, where she poured the gin out onto the ground several stories below. Most of the gin evaporated during the freefall. She then placed the empty glass on a tray held by a passing waiter.

In her stroll, Lizzy had not gone unnoticed by several men. A few brought her a drink, which she refused with silence and a wave of her hand.

Eventually, the producer found her on the balcony and offered her another gin. She accepted it and sipped. She immediately knew he had spiked the drink because of her experience at the Blind Pig in Indianapolis and some Chicago parties.

The producer said, "Drink up baby-doll. You'll enjoy the party so much more."

Lizzy nodded but didn't take another sip. Instead, she decided to distract the producer by stroking his ego. With a sideways glance, she asked, "How much do parties cost you?"

He grinned and looked around the balcony and said, "You don't want to know, but it is a lot. It's worth it, though, to help everyone unwind." He reached for her bare shoulder, but Lizzy brushed his hand away. "Oh, my young lady, you must lighten up if you are going to get anywhere in this town."

At the moment, one of the flappers gave a loud "Whoop," causing many men to look at her. As the producer turned and stared to see where the outburst came from, Lizzy reached over the balcony and dumped her drink. When the producer turned back to Lizzy, he saw her remove the empty glass from her lips.

He smiled when he saw that and said, "Now you are getting into the spirit. The place is beginning to gain some momentum." He reached for Lizzy's hand to lead her to the dance floor. Lizzy hated herself for letting him lead her. She hated every second of it as the producer leered at her. Once, she thought he positioned himself to see down the front of her dress. She wanted to slap him. Instead, she quit dancing and stood motionless. Eventually, he looked at her face and followed where her eyes stared. She looked at Frank walking hand-in-hand with a woman into a back room. She gawked. Seeing his chance to wedge into Lizzy's relationship with Frank, he said, "Well, I know where they are going. I guess men will be men."

Lizzy started to run to Frank, but the producer put an arm around her waist and restricted her. He looked away from Frank and the woman and said, "Frank always gets what Frank wants."

Lizzy's mind spun. She assumed Frank had cheated on her when he traveled, but she never thought he would do it so openly. Immediately, Lizzy decided to drink. A waiter passed by, and she grabbed two gins, shot one down, and placed the empty glass back on the waiter's tray. She bit her lip and watched Frank and the women disappear into the back room.

Like so many men had done before, the producer placed his hand on Lizzy's bottom. She pushed him away and said, "Not now and not ever."

He stepped closer to her and said, "You need to be with someone. Some women have been raped at mushing parties."

At that, Lizzy turned and sped out to the balcony. Seeing the man start to follow her, she said, "Don't follow me, and I won't create a scene that will embarrass you."

Turning away from the event, Lizzy thought of it as an orgy. She would learn the next day the producer had raped a woman later during the party. Of course, no one could prove it because of the status difference between the producer and the woman, who was only an extra for a film. Many of the higher-up men considered it was the extra's duty to entertain them. After all, they allowed the women to drink alcohol and consume drugs for free.

Lizzy didn't know how long she leaned against the balcony wall, but four men walked up to her, and two placed a hand in an inappropriate place. She chased them away. With a mean look on her face, they knew she meant business. Sick of the entire mess, she decided to leave Hollywood, with or without Frank.

When she stepped back into the ballroom, she saw Frank and the woman return from the back room. Frank stopped and saw Lizzy as he rearranged his pants. Lizzy's jaw dropped because she recognized the woman as the prostitute to whom she had handed the $80 a few days ago. To Frank, Lizzy's stare seemed frozen in time. In reality, her stare lasted only a second because she turned and ran to the front entrance. Frank motioned for the Caddy driver, who stood by the door, to stop her, but Lizzy slipped out the door before the Caddy driver knew what Frank wanted. Outside, she hailed a taxi, but the driver caught up with her and waved the taxi passed.

He turned to Lizzy and said, "A taxi won't be necessary. I will take you back to the Roosevelt."

Frank had caught up with the man and Lizzy and told her, "We will go back together." Frank gently grabbed her arm, but she wouldn't have anything to do with it and pulled her arm out of his grasp. Once in the Cadillac, the fight began. Frank knew Lizzy saw him with the prostitute and stated, "Nothing happened."

Lizzy snapped, "Then why were you rearranging your pants when you walked out?"

Frank knew he was busted but tried to pull off the impossible and make Lizzy think he had done nothing. "She wanted to show off her acting skills and see if I could help her get a part in an upcoming production. She got carried away."

"That woman is a prostitute, Frank." Lizzy hesitated because she didn't want to admit to Frank she had wandered out of the Roosevelt by herself when he was gone. After a moment, she said, "I found her in one of the filthiest allies I've ever seen."

Frank immediately turned to the Caddy driver and said, "You took her down an alley?"

The driver started to explain, but Lizzy cut him off. "He didn't take me anywhere. I hailed a taxi to see the town this Caddy driver never showed me. I visited a cooperative for women who had no luck and no reason to be in Hollywood. I made the taxi driver go down the alley to see it for myself."

"Baby, you shouldn't have gone, especially by yourself."

"Don't 'baby' me, Frank. You are still in a lot of hot water." She stayed quiet for the rest of the trip. Frank took his cue from her and sat silently.

At the Roosevelt, Lizzy grabbed a glass of moonshine, strode into the second bedroom of their suite, and slammed the door shut. Frank figured it was best to let her cool off overnight.

By morning, she had cooled off, but she had determined during the night to leave Hollywood. When the hotel waiter delivered breakfast, Lizzy and Frank sat together at a table by a window. She looked out the window at the city. Then she said, "What you did last night was wrong. On top of that, you disrespected me in front of the others. I had to fight off one man after another at the party, partially because you left me." Silent for a moment, she added, "I will not participate in an industry that abuses women so badly."

Frank started to protest.

Lizzy said, "Don't. I've had my eyes opened, and I won't stand for it." Frank could see the change in her entire countenance and feared, for the first time, he would lose Lizzy.

"What do you propose?"

"This is not a proposal, Frank. I demand to leave Hollywood."

Frank calculated the loss in money and reputation a retreat from Hollywood would cost the Chicago Outfit. He knew he would be held accountable, but he agreed to her terms.

Lizzy added, "I will return to acting in Chicago."

"Babe, please give it a week."

Lizzy pounded the table and exclaimed, "I will not give it another day. I want out."

Any other woman would have suffered Frank's rath by making such a demand. Lizzy was not any other woman to Frank, who knew he had done wrong. If dropping out was his only option, he would take the option.

"Well, we will have to cancel your part in the film. Are you sure you want to throw your Hollywood career away?"

"I'd rather throw my life away than condone horrid behavior."

Frank said, "I will talk to the producer."

"No!" Lizzy demanded. "I'll talk to him."

By afternoon, Lizzy walked into the producer's office without an appointment. Smiling, he looked Lizzy up and down. "To what do I owe this pleasant surprise?"

"To your behavior and the behavior of almost every man in the industry. You are a pig. You disgust me."

The producer stood quickly and said, "I will not tolerate your attitude while we work on this film together."

"You won't have to. I quit, and I'm leaving this damnable city."

He stared at Lizzy, and then a wry smile crossed his face. "You can't; we have a contract."

"You voided the contract when you sexually violated my existence."

"That's hardly a contract breaker, especially here in Hollywood."

"Then you broke it when you raped the extra."

The producer stood frozen and silent. The statement took him back so quickly he blurted out, "How do you know about that?" He instantly regretted his question because it incompetently confirmed what Lizzy knew to be true.

"Word gets around town, especially among us women." Lizzy turned to the door, but before she walked out, she pointed at the producer, "You won't say anything. You won't stop me, or I'll bring on the rape charges."

The producer had never dealt with a woman of such resolve and force. It left him speechless as she walked away. He never saw her again.

Chapter 14

June 2

Before Frank could arrange the trip back to Chicago, the L.A. correspondent for the Chicago City Times found Frank and Lizzy's room at the Roosevelt. He knocked on the door, which Lizzy hesitantly opened because Frank was gone arranging for transportation.

Lizzy recognized the reporter because he had interviewed her before. Even though she liked him, she started to close the door on him because she didn't want to see another man at that moment. He simply said, "Wait. I know the story, but I want to hear it from you."

Lizzy held the door and said, "What do you know?"

"Can I come in?" She knew he had a sincere heart and mind. Still, she hesitated but eventually opened the door more to let him in. She wore a slip dress, which the reporter took in with a glance as she walked across the room and onto the balcony. She pointed to a wrought iron chair and said, "Have a seat."

Sitting on the balcony, they began what would be the interview of his life.

"So, what did you hear?"

The reporter interjected, "This conversation will be on the record, right?"

"Sure."

"Well, I know you, for some reason, kissed off the biggest contract in Hollywood. I know Frank is with the Chicago Outfit. And, I know you two are leaving Hollywood."

"There you have it. You have your story. So why are you here?" She stood and walked to the bar inside the room. The reporter followed her every move with his eyes while he bit his lip because he'd never seen someone so beautiful. At the bar, Lizzy mixed champagne and orange juice. She saw the reporter and held a glass up to indicate she would bring him a drink. He accepted.

She handed him the drink when she returned to the balcony and sat back down. Many thoughts ran through her mind. The reporter had been one of the sweetest and most admirable men she had met in

Hollywood. Because Frank had just betrayed her, she thought about cheating on Frank with the lovely young man before her. While the thought impetuously crossed her mind, Lizzy didn't think of herself as a vengeful person, so she dismissed the whim. Looking out over the balcony, she wondered if she caught a wisp of air with the Callery Pear smell. She decided she did not. She wondered what to say next and how it would affect her when she returned to Chicago. While her thoughts ran wild, it seemed like an eternity since she asked the reporter, "So why are you here?"

In reality, and to the reporter, it was only a moment. Having accepted the drink, he raised his glass and said, "I want to hear your side of the story."

Both still seated, Lizzy clinked her glass to his and said, "That's a unique concept here in Hollywood." She hesitated and then said, "Okay, the next part is off the record, and if you use it, I will deny it and tear you to shreds."

The reporter gulped. He had never heard a woman as bold as Lizzy. He set his pencil down and raised his arms with his hands wide open. He had an innocent face Lizzy loved but didn't let him know.

She continued, "Hollywood is lecherous. The men who use women and the women who allow the men to do so make me sick." They sat quietly for a moment. Then she added, "This you can use." He picked up his pencil. "Hollywood and I don't agree. I love the Chicago theater, and I will return there. I'll never work in this town again."

He wrote every word and considered what she said. Then he said, "There are women who would die to have what you had."

Lizzy looked over the balcony again and said, "Or screw anyone for what I had."

The reporter's eyes widened as he looked Lizzy over.

"Don't report that."

He shook his head and said, "I won't, but I know what you mean." Then he asked, "How does it feel?"

Lizzy's face questioned him. "How does what feel?"

"How does it feel telling Hollywood to go…," he hesitated but then blurted out, "…telling Hollywood to go to hell?"

"Liberating. You can use that."

They chatted for a few more minutes, and then the reporter said, "Well, I have a deadline and must go."

Lizzy reached out and put a hand on his and said, "Please treat me with respect, right!"

Without hesitation, the reporter pursed his lips and nodded affirmatively.

Chapter 15

June 1928

Fritz sat at the dinner table with the rest of the Hoffmans and Amelia. "Hey, here's a new word for the day!" He chimed. "It's 'astronaut.'"

"As what?" Berta chimed in.

"Astronaut. The article says mankind will send people up into space and to the moon in the future. What do you think of that?"

"I'm skeptical," Karl spoke up. "Who wants to go into space? You can't farm it." He looked at Fritz, who had turned red with rage. "Hey, what's up with you?"

Fritz gawked at the next article in the newspaper and then slammed it to the table, causing Amelia to jump. Karl reached across the table and pulled the newspaper toward himself, wondering what could have made Fritz change moods so quickly. He opened it up and glanced around the two pages in front of him. Then he spotted it. "Well, I'll be." He looked at Fritz and continued, "Do you mind if I read it aloud?" Without a word, Fritz gestured to indicate Karl could proceed.

Karl read the headline, "Stage actress rebukes Hollywood. The subhead reads: Lizzy Lee Returns to Chicago." The family looked at Fritz. Karl continued to tell the family what the article said.

"It appears Lizzy was to star in a silent movie, but just before filming, she left Hollywood and said she'd never return. It quotes her saying, 'Hollywood and I don't agree. I love the Chicago theater, and I will return there. I'll never work in this town again.'"

"The reporter goes on to say Lizzy is associated with the Chicago Outfit." The story didn't relate to whether that was good or bad. Al Capone was still viewed as a Robin Hood by many. Karl went on to say, "Didn't Bar have a run-in with them in Lafayette?"

Fritz nodded.

Karl looked at Fritz and said, "Sorry, buddy."

Berta, who had walked by Fritz, patted his shoulder and asked, "Are you okay?"

Fritz mumbled, "She is in the past, and I'm beyond her." No one in the room believed him, but they didn't say anything.

Two days later, Frank and Lizzy completed their return to Chicago. Capone quickly called for Frank to visit him in his office. Capone was fit to be tied.

"Do you realize what your actions mean?" He asked. Frank started to talk, but Capone put his hand out to shut him up. "Aside from the money you cost us, you will never return to Hollywood again. I'll have to work doubly hard to reassure producers this will never happen again. Where is the woman?"

Capone let Frank talk for the first time since he began yelling at him. "She's at my house. Look, I take the blame, not her. I don't want to lose her."

Capone huffed. "You are lucky the steel move you made brings in the big bucks." He hesitated. "Otherwise, I don't know what I'd have done with you."

Frank said, "It probably would have involved a set of concrete shoes and Lake Michigan, I suppose."

Capone slowly shook his head. He loved Frank like a brother, but he was so upset with him at the moment. "All this for a pair of tits."

It turned out Lizzy didn't stay at home. Instead, she went to the Auditorium Theater to visit Paul Elman. She found him in the theater sitting three rows from the stage. While Lizzy walked down to the row he was sitting in; she listened to an actor on stage reciting words from a play she had stared in last year. The man finished and stood looking at Elman. Just then, Lizzy turned into the row where Elman sat. A smile grew on his face when he saw Lizzy, but he turned to the actor on stage and said. "That's enough for now. Very good, and thank you. You can go now."

Lizzy walked up to Elman and said, "I could recite the lines between his if you want to hear more."

Elman stood and held Lizzy's outstretched hands. "That's quite unnecessary, my dear. How are you?"

"Well, time will tell. Frank is meeting with Capone as we speak."

"No, how are you really? You!"

"To be honest, I'm trying to find myself again. Hollywood was so disgusting. I couldn't believe I was there." Elman tilted his head, rubbed his chin, and looked at her through the top of his spectacles. Lizzy continued, "I know, you warned me. What is wrong with the world where people treat others so poorly?"

"Have a seat," Elman gestured to a seat, and she sat next to him. They held hands while they sat. "So, the town hasn't changed much."

Lizzy wrinkled her brow and said, "You surely didn't think they would change much in only a few years."

"Maybe someday, women will call out those men, and we will see a real change."

"Not in our lifetime, I suppose,"

"Hey, you made the news. Everybody who's anybody read your story. I heard it went nationwide. Maybe it will influence some reform."

Lizzy rolled her eyes. "I'm afraid the lechery is too ingrained for change."

They sat silently for a moment, reflecting on the situation.

"But hey, you're back in Chicago. That's good news for our theater!"

"I can't wait. What's in the works?"

Elman shared the details of what the Auditorium had planned. One included an off-Broadway production of *Lady, Be Good*. He said, "You'll be perfect in it."

Chapter 16

Frank couldn't believe he received only a lecture from Capone. Still, he called the others with the Northwest Indiana Outfit and told them they needed a retreat to discuss moving forward. He emphasized they should bring their Goomahs. Frank was in trouble with his crew because they felt he had undermined Capone. He reassured them he was not in trouble and said, "We will partially have a retreat and partially have a party on me." He instructed them to go to Miller's Point in Indiana. He told them he would bring the hooch and other supplies.

When he returned to his Chicago home, he felt confused and angry because he didn't find Lizzy. He avoided putting out a search party for her because it would make him look weak. After all, he couldn't control his woman. Instead, he sent the Caddy driver to the warehouse to pick up liquor and drugs for the retreat. Frank packed two suitcases. One for Lizzy and another for himself. He wanted to leave as soon as she returned. He never dreamed she might not return.

After Frank had drunk some moonshine, an hour later, Lizzy walked in the door. Fuming, he exclaimed, "Where have you been?"

Lizzy set her purse on the console by the door. She looked at Frank and said, "It's a little early to be drinking, isn't it?"

"Never mind that. Where have you been?"

"At the Auditorium. I'm lining up work. Is that okay?"

"I was worried about you."

"Worried I'd leave you?" She walked over to Frank and sat on the wing of the chair where he sat. Frank naturally draped an arm on Lizzy's legs. She continued, "Look, I know we had a bad time in Hollywood, but now we are in Chicago. I love it here. You brought me home, and I'm willing to start anew." She softly touched his chin.

She asked, "How about you? Let's start over."

"I suppose. How'd things go at the Auditorium?"

"Very well. I'm sure I have a part in a new off-Broadway play."

Taken back, Frank cocked his head to the side and said, "How do you do that?"

"Do what?"

"You walk into people's lives and get whatever you want."

Lizzy stood and patted him on the shoulder and said, "I guess it's my personality," she laughed for a second and then wore a somber expression. "It hasn't always been that way, Frank."

Frank watched her walk away and said, "Maybe it's your ass getting you what you want."

She took off her gloves and turned to look at Frank, "Only you get that." Then she admonished him, "I wish I could say the same for me."

While it hurt Frank's feelings, it reassured him of Lizzy's loyalty. That was exactly her intent.

When she stepped into the next room, she asked, "What are these bags doing here?"

Frank waved his drink in the air and said, "We are leaving. Tonight, we will be at Miller's Point for the first night of a retreat."

"Just you and me?"

"No, the whole Northwest crew will be there."

"It won't be a pretty scene. How did it go with Capone?"

"I'm still alive, and I'm fine. You haven't made him happy, but don't worry, everything else is fine. You and I will never go back to Hollywood. He's going out there to settle things down. It will do him good to...." Frank almost said, '...to wet his noodle.' He realized the word choice was wrong, so he shut up and drank the rest of his hooch.

The Caddy driver stepped into the house and said, "I set everything up, even the groceries. When do you want to leave?"

Frank stood, tenderly laid his hand on Lizzy's shoulders, and said, "Freshen up doll-face, and we will head south in a few minutes." He pointed to the bags and told the driver to put them in the Caddy.

On the drive, Frank pointed at businesses with whom he had ties. He began to describe those ties, which was the first time Frank opened up about his work, other than the illegal moonshine.

Surprising Frank, Lizzy asked, "You don't run any whorehouses, do you?"

Frank's silence disturbed Lizzy until he said, "Those aren't under my rule if that's what you mean."

Lizzy was not ecstatic about Frank's revelation and didn't pursue it further.

Within a few miles, they passed by the Indiana town of Morocco. A curious sign had a pair of red boots on it. Frank smiled and said, "Well, it's an interesting story. The founders named Morocco after the country in Northern Africa or a traveler's Moroccan red boots. As the story goes, the leather on the boots was like no other anyone had ever seen in these parts. A local asked the traveler where he obtained the boots. He said only one word, 'Morocco.'"

Lizzy jumped in, "So they called the town Morocco, which ties in with the country and the boots. How do you know these things?"

Frank said, "It's my job to know everything I can about Northwest Indiana and Chicago."

As they drove on, Lizzy began to see the prairie land of Indiana juxtaposed with the woodland to the east. She felt comfortable going back home to Indiana.

Chapter 17

July 1928

From the day Lizzy walked to the Hoffman farm, Fritz barely talked to Lizzy. The two sat on the porch minutes before sunset. Berta told the rest of the family to stay off the porch. "Let them have a little time alone. Maybe they can patch things up."

Karl rolled his eyes and said, "Fat chance."

In front of Fritz and Lizzy, the horizon sparkled with bright hues and with wisps of white clouds, yellow streaks of light, and blue sky across the land. Wafts of fresh, clean tangy, and earthy aromas graced the couple sitting on the porch. A luscious green pasture spread out in front of them where reddish-gold Gelbvieh cattle and calves stood munching on the alfalfa. The Hoffman's did well with the land and the farm that Fritz's great grandfather bought for one dollar per acre.

Lizzy told Fritz how much she adored John's Jardin Botanique. Fritz stayed silent and wondered when the others would come out to the porch.

Lizzy continued, "This porch and view of the prairie are amazing."

Fritz chimed in, "Isn't too simple after all you've seen?"

"On the contrary, it is perfect." She looked at Fritz straight on and touched his knee. "Look, I know what I did to you was horrible. I can only ask you to forgive me. You have to understand your family has shown me my ways were wrong. I apologize to you. Do you think you could ever love me again?" Lizzy didn't know why she blurted that out, except she was nervous and rambling.

Fritz looked her in the eyes for the first time since she came to the Hoffman farm. He melted inside because her beauty always stirred him. Without touching her, he replied in the form of a question, "Love?" He repeated the word, "Love? You don't get to use the love word around me. I loved you. Maybe deep down inside, I still love you."

Lizzy responded by putting both hands on his knees.

Fritz waved a hand in the air. "But let me put an end to your pursuit right now. I don't trust you, and I never will." He gently moved her hands from his knees. "Without trust, love is a vague concept for me."

Lizzy put her hands to her face and cried. For the first time, she realized how much she had hurt Fritz. Calming herself, she simply said, "I see."

They sat quietly for a moment more.

"Can you accept my apology?"

"I can, but please understand I cannot give you any more." Little did Fritz know he would give her much, much more.

The sun sank closer to the horizon. Lizzy watched it and took in the fresh air blowing across the field in front of them. She smirked when she compared the smell of the Callery Pear tree with the scent of the pasture. They both took a start as Bar came around the corner of the porch and announced, "I'm here. Let the party begin!" He held up a jug of moonshine, which Lizzy had not tasted since she left Fritz.

Having seen Bar drive up the lane, Karl looked at his mother and said, "Well, that reunion is over. We might as well join them on the porch." When he approached Lizzy, Bar, and Fritz, seated in the rockers, he handed them each a glass for Bar's hooch. Bar readily poured the drinks but had his eyes glued on Lizzy.

Karl asked Lizzy and Fritz how the reunion went. Instantly Fritz realized the family had purposely not joined the pair on the porch. He frowned and shook his head at Karl. "We got some things worked out."

Finally realizing Bar was instantly infatuated with Lizzy, Fritz said, "Bar, this is Lizzy Lee, and please don't drool on her." Pointing at Bar, Fritz said, "Lizzy, this is Bar. It's a shorter nickname than his real name, Brian Allen Ryan. You can drool on him. I don't care."

They all raised their glasses and clinked them together.

Fritz continued, "You are drinking the same moonshine you drank at the Blind Pig, and Bar is the one who makes it."

Karl chimed in, "Here's to Bar."

Bar stared at Lizzy but said nothing. Lizzy felt uncomfortable, so she scooted her rocker a little farther from Bar.

Karl said to Lizzy, "He's harmless." Then he slapped Bar on the back and said, "She does talk. You can do more than stare at her." The quip loosened the group, and they started drinking in earnest. Soon the rest of the family joined them, young Patrick and Samuel moved to the sandbox. Fritz quickly told Karl, "It's your turn to clean them up when we head in." The older brothers took on the tradition of cleaning the boys up because they usually stayed out later than the women.

Lizzy wore a puzzled look, so Karl explained they all took turns cleaning up the boys from the sandpile before going into the house for the night. She smiled and said, "It sounds like fun. Karl, I will help."

The sun started to touch the horizon. Lizzy said, "It is so beautiful now with specks of red and gold splashing the earth in its brilliance."

Amelia asked, "With all you've seen in Hollywood and Chicago, I'd think our sunset would be pretty boring."

"The old Lizzy would have thought so too, but your family has shown me how much I missed in life before." She looked at her almost empty glass, and Bar immediately stood up and refilled it. "When I arrived here, I told you I would explain someday why Frank and the Outfit were so upset with me. It might as well be now."

She explained she could not stand the way people treated each other in Hollywood, especially how men treated young, innocent women.

Karl interrupted, "We read you didn't like Hollywood and moved back to Chicago to act. How is that going?"

"It isn't now after I ran away from the gang. I cannot show my face in Chicago again. I wrote a letter to a contact up there and told him I had left Frank and could not come back." She saw Fritz's stern look and said, "I didn't put a return address on the letter. Amelia mailed it from Lafayette so that no one would know I'm here near Boulton." Lizzy took Fritz's look as an objection against her mailing a letter to Chicago. Instead, it was a pang of rage or jealousy when she said, "I told HIM."

Amelia said, "I'll drink to that, but you were headed somewhere. What were you going to explain?"

Lizzy nodded and swirled her drink. "Before I say more, I want to point out you folks drink and enjoy life."

John held up his glass of lemonade and said, "Yes, we do." John, who had been a hefty drinker right after serving in the big war, quit the instant a war buddy suggested he rebuild the Jardin.

Lizzy tipped her glass to John. "That's just it. In Hollywood and Chicago, people drink mostly to use other people. I watched dirty old men get women drunk to have sex with them. I've witnessed one man get another man drunk so he could swindle him."

Berta shook her head slowly in disgust at the thought.

"That's why I left Hollywood, but it wasn't good timing for the Outfit. I left just before producing a movie where I was the leading lady. The Outfit invested much in me and the movie I almost made, all of which they lost when I left."

Somehow, Lizzy's confession lightened Fritz's attitude toward her. On the other hand, Bar listened to every word Lizzy said as if it came from the Bible. Karl was still amused with Bar.

"Anyway, my leaving Hollywood caused big problems for Frank. It led to him threatening me with a knife the night we went to Miller's Point."

Finally, Bar snapped to attention and said, "Ain't no reason a man should do that." Berta agreed, also amused at Bar's obvious infatuation for Lizzy.

John said, "Well, here you are at the Hoffman home. You are safe here."

Lizzy shook her head, "I hope you are right. And, I dearly hope I've not put you all into jeopardy."

Bar blurted out, "I had a run-in with the Outfit a few years ago. I put them in their place." He looked at the Hoffmans, Amelia, and Lizzy. "We will protect you."

Lizzy held her glass up and pointed to the sunset, where it painted a solid orange band as the sun had slipped below the horizon. "Thank you!" She said, "Thank you for allowing me to share your glorious evening with you."

Chapter 18

July /August

Bar became more interested in Hoffman's sunsets since he met Lizzy. He invited himself to join them on the porch two evenings per week for a couple of weeks. He would have visited more, but the summer chores kept the men busy in the field. Of course, he always brought the moonshine. One night he asked Lizzy if she would like to see how they make it. She accepted the invitation. She now knew Bar for what he was, a big, kind-hearted man with more innocence than one would expect from a moonshiner.

Bar jumped up from the rocker and held a hand out to Lizzy, who smiled slightly because of Bar's eagerness. Bar took her hand and told Frank, "We shall be back within the hour."

Lizzy hesitated and asked, "We are not going into Boulton, are we?"

"No, my still is at Moonshine's farm in the middle of nowhere."

Lizzy looked puzzled. Fritz said, "Bar's boss's nickname is Moonshine Moore, well…" he hesitated and then said, "…because he started a moonshine business."

Lizzy nodded and said, "Good because I don't want to go anywhere one of Frank's goons might see me."

Happily, Lizzy climbed into Bar's Model T pickup. Bar backed the truck up and turned it around; they glowed inside the pickup because the residual sunlight perfectly spotlighted the two souls like actors on a stage.

"Well, there's something I never thought I'd see," Berta said with a smile. "Bar with a beautiful young woman and obviously the love of his life."

Karl said, "You are always the matchmaker, mom."

Berta added, "It is love that makes the world go around. And his is so obvious. I wonder if she will let him in."

Frank became obsessed with finding Lizzy, even though Capone told him to forget her. Frank's pursuit was unflinching. He drove to Miller's Point every other weekend to see if Lizzy had come back. When he returned empty-handed, he grew more livid with Lizzy. Likewise, Capone grew tired of Frank's search but didn't say anything as long as Frank conducted his primary business.

A month after the night Lizzy disappeared and unsure of what he would do about Lizzy, Frank commanded one of the Goomahs, who knew Lizzy, to go to every town within 50 miles of Miller's Point. He paid for her to stay in each town for four days and scout to find Lizzy. With so many small towns in Indiana, it took months before anyone from the Outfit would show up in Boulton.

At Moonshine's still, Bar eagerly showed Lizzy the mechanics, but not the process which he tried to maintain as a secret. He had poured them each a drink as they viewed the moonshine shed. Bar adored how well Lizzy held her liquor. "Most girls are trashed with one or two drinks."

Lizzy looked at the still and said, "I'm not a girl. I'm a woman."

"A damn fine one at that."

Lizzy turned and looked at Bar. "Do you tell all the women that?"

Bar touched her chin, which Lizzy allowed, and said, "Until you, there was no woman I wanted to be with."

"So, tell me, how do you want to be with me?"

His answer shocked Lizzy because it didn't involve anything sexual. Bar said, "For the rest of my life."

"You sure it's not only momentary lust, and you want to capture me as a sexual win."

Bar squirmed a bit. "Don't tell Karl or Fritz, but I'm not that type of man." He put his hand on the still. "I am a one lady man, and until you came to the Hoffman farm, I had not met that woman."

"You are a virgin?" Lizzy spoke the question very delicately.

Bar bit his lips and sheepishly nodded yes.

His words and actions moved Lizzy. But still, she said, "I've had many men react to me the way you have. How can I know what you really feel?"

Bar turned toward the wall for a moment and then returned and gazed at Lizzy. "I'm sure you've had many outstanding men who wanted to court you so they could put another notch on their holster, but I won't." Lizzy felt she might have hurt Bar's feelings. Bar put his hands on his hips even though he wanted to put them on, Lizzy. Finally, he asked her, "Do you know what love is?"

"I don't know if I've ever seen it or felt it."

"I have the moment I laid eyes on you."

"That's lust."

"Wait. Before judging me, listen to what I have to say about love. Lust is temporary. I know many men who have felt only lust. I'm not the man who simply wants sex to fulfill an empty life. Love is filled with dedication and determination to care for one individual for the rest of your life. It's about caring for someone as much or more than yourself. It isn't fleeting."

Bar's words shocked Lizzy. She never expected those words out of Bar. She wondered how she hadn't seen this side of him earlier. She was the target of lust from many men, and she simply expected it from Bar. After a moment, she said, "Well, I suppose we should go back to the Hoffmans."

Bar smiled and said, "I am so happy we had a moment alone."

When they climbed back into the Model T, Lizzy scooted a little closer to Bar and kissed him on the cheek, and then she looked at him. She said, "Most men would be groping me right now." She smiled as if she was permitting him.

"No, ma'am, not me. I'm willing to wait until I can convince you I'm the one for you."

Lizzy sat back in the pickup and quietly said, "You've done an amazing amount of convincing tonight."

They returned to the Hoffmans, who were still sitting on the porch gazing at the stars. In the clear rural night sky, stars dotted and shined through the blackness at the edges. In the middle of the sky, the stars thickened and painted it milky white.

Lizzy looked at Karl and said, "Oh my goodness, are Patrick and Sammy inside? I wanted to help you clean them up again tonight."

Karl snickered, "You have done great so far, and there will be plenty of opportunities in the future."

Bar and Lizzy drank one more glassful of the moonshine. As they did, John and Berta excused themselves, went into the house, and prepared for bed. Soon, Fritz, Bar, and Lizzy were the only ones on the porch.

Fritz earnestly asked, "Did you learn anything about the moonshine business tonight?"

"It's fascinating."

When they had returned from the trip, Fritz immediately saw the change in both of them. Bar was happier than he ever had been, and Lizzy was not so stand-offish toward Bar.

After a few more sips, Lizzy stood and put a hand on Bar's shoulder and said, "Goodnight."

The men watched her walk around the corner of the porch. Allowing more time for Lizzy to go inside, Fritz asked Bar, "Do you know what you are doing?"

He nodded affirmatively. Fritz took his last drink for the night, "You cannot trust her."

Bar looked at Fritz, "She's had a tough life. Your family has had a beautiful impact on her. She's a different Lizzy now than when you met her."

Fritz nodded, "Time will tell, but be very careful, my friend."

Time did tell the story of Bar and Lizzy; by August, Bar won her over to his way of thinking. Lizzy enjoyed him immensely, unlike other men she had been with who tried to win her over for lust. She toyed with sexual exploration with Bar, but because of his innocence, she did not pressure him. Bar's courting became a unique feeling in her life. She wanted to be around Bar, but she didn't need an evening filled with sex. At least not yet.

Lizzy could count the men she trusted on one hand. Fritz, Paul Elman, and the Chicago City News reporter were indeed up there on the trust meter. It surprised her when Bar climbed ahead of those three so quickly. While Lizzy adjusted to rural life, Bar became her guide. The Hoffmans continued to dote on her, except for Fritz. She grew more and more confident in her relationship with Bar. It had been two months since they met. She had usually slept with most men within two days, let alone two months.

One day she thought the time had come because Bar visited the Hoffman farm when he knew some of them had gone into town. Karl and Fritz stayed busy with the chores.

Hat in hand and with no moonshine, Bar knocked on the door. He was sure Lizzy would answer, so he waited to speak to her. She did, and Bar stammered for a moment. The awkwardness was not sexual; it was about a question Bar wanted to ask Lizzy.

Still not saying much, he pointed to two rockers on the porch. Lizzy followed suit and took a seat. "Bar, what is it?" She asked. "You look as nervous as a rabbit hunted by a dog." She hesitated because she never thought she would use a hick phrase; she smiled at him and placed a hand on his shoulder.

Bar said, "I'm trying to ask you a question, but it's difficult for me and, I hope, not too embarrassing for you."

"It's okay, Bar. Ask away."

Bar straightened in his seat, where he towered over Lizzy. "Well, you know I love you. I-I hope someday you can love me. I know you're not there yet, but I think…" Bar hesitated, and then he exclaimed, "…will you move in with me? I know over time you will come to love me." Then he blushed and said, "I'm not talking sex right now. It can come with time too."

Lizzy smiled, and for the second time since she met Bar, she kissed him on the cheek. She said, "It's a big move."

"Sure, but I think it is the next step. I know it's the right thing to do if we take time to learn more about each other."

"I think it is a wonderful time to do so," I only ask that you give me time to talk with Berta. She has been so lovely to me. I want to seek her approval."

Bar began to relax because he spat out the big question and put it behind him. He looked around and saw Karl and Fritz walking out of the barn and approaching the couple on the porch. Lizzy quietly whispered to Bar, "Let me talk to Berta before we tell anyone else."

Bar nodded.

Lizzy noted the boys smelled like the barn but didn't mention it.

Karl looked at Bar and said, "What, no moonshine?"

"Didn't bring it."

"Well, Fritz and I are done with the chores. I'm going into the house and getting some moonshine." As he stepped toward the front door, he turned and asked, "Who else?"

The other three raised their hands.

Karl said with moonshine cups in hand, "Here's to good times." Then he noticed Lizzy lightly clinked her cup into Bars. 'Strange,' he thought, but he didn't pursue it.

Chapter 19

September 1928

After Lizzy moved in with Bar, she helped with meals and chores around the house. Berta and Amelia had taught Lizzy the basics of cooking to satisfy a man's appetite. Over time, they would teach her more of the art of prairie cooking.

Every evening, Bar and Lizzy sat and talked at the dinner table or near the fireplace on cooler evenings. They slept in separate rooms. Sometimes while Bar worked the farm or still, and Lizzy tended to house cleaning and made their beds, she would sit for a long time on

Bar's bed. She sometimes brought the sheet to her face to take in his scent. While it wasn't cologne-scented like Frank's or some of the men she slept with in Indianapolis, it was Bar, a man through and through.

By October, Lizzy felt guilty she wasn't contributing enough. Bar never even considered that she needed to pay her way. They both felt as if she should stay away from Boulton in case Frank searched for her there. Occasionally, they visited the Hoffmans.

One morning, Lizzy walked to the shed, which was closer to Moonshine's house. Inside, Bar busied himself with the moonshine-making process. Not sure if Bar welcomed her in the shop, she peered in the door. She asked, "Can I help?"

Bar looked at Moonshine with a questioning look.

Moonshine said, "Let her come in."

Lizzy jumped at the chance and quickly moved to Bar's side. Of course, Moonshine looked Lizzy up and down and said, "I don't know if you are hardy enough for this line of work. You're as skinny as a bean pole." Lizzy didn't mind him calling her a bean pole. She put her arms at her sides, fluttered her hands, and twirled as the men watched. "You're definitely a distraction." Moonshine concluded. "But in a good way. You can stay."

Lizzy loved the shed. It was warmer than the house when it was cold outside because of the heat to boil the liquids, and it supplied the drink people loved.

Bar watched her nose around. He said, "Well if you are going to help, you need to learn something about it."

He explained the alcohol they produced came from the British term 'moonshining' because most people conducted the illegal process at night with the windows blocked so no one could see the light.

He said, "We are so rural and hidden; we don't have to hide it at night."

Moonshine added, "Plus, the sheriff loves this stuff, so he looks the other way."

Taking a break from what he did, Bar explained, "There are two processes in making moonshine, fermentation and distillation. In fermentation, we convert sugar into acids, gases, and alcohol. There's a sequence in distillation. It starts with heating, evaporating, cooling, and finally condensing." Bar impressed Lizzy with his knowledge and clear explanation. He continued, "The recipe is cornmeal," he patted on a burlap bag of the meal he and Moonshine had filled a few days ago. He continued we add, "yeast, sugar, and water. That's the basics of it. Oh, and we keep the equipment very clean, so we don't ruin the end product."

Lizzy ran her hand down a smooth copper tank and said, "Everyone loves your moonshine. What makes it different?"

Moonshine swelled with pride when people bragged about his moonshine. "Okay, you will now become the second person in the world who will know my secret." He pointed at Bar with his thumb to indicate he was the other person. "It's the cornmeal, the water, the copper tanks, and the extreme cleanliness Bar mentioned. We are blessed with the best of corn and water than anywhere around. Almost all of the corn I grow goes into hooch."

Bar hefted a bag of cornmeal onto his shoulder and poured it into a vat. When he finished, he said, "I need to go upstairs to grab some jar lids and jugs. Care to join me?"

Lizzy said, "Sure. She followed behind him as they climbed up the ladder on the wall." The bashful Bar went first so he wouldn't look up at Lizzy's legs as they climbed.

Once upstairs, Bar pointed to a small box and asked, "Do you mind grabbing a box of lids?" When she bent over, she, partially by accident and partially on purpose, rubbed her derriere against Bar's crotch. Bar froze for a moment but then gently reached out for her. Lizzy didn't resist. Slowly Bar ducked down and kissed Lizzy on the lips. He was far from delivering the perfect kiss, but it warmed them immensely.

He lifted the box from her hands and set it aside. They embraced, with Bar holding her tightly. Lizzy thought, 'I'll need to teach him something about kissing, but I certainly love the power of his embrace.'

She leaned back after the long kiss, looked at Bar, and said, "It took you long enough."

Bar smiled and quietly said, "It was torture, but worth the wait." Then he placed a flat hand on her back and lowered her onto the straw.

Bar had no idea what to expect or do for his first-time making love. His desire drove him, so he followed his instinct. Although Lizzy had thought he needed to work on his kisses, she soon realized he needed no help in the sex department.

Moonshine could hear Lizzy moaning from the loft. He shook his head and mumbled, "She is no Quaker like most women around here."

When Bar and Lizzy climbed down from the loft, Moonshine said, "It sure took you long enough. Did you get lost?" Then he looked at Bar's empty hands and asked, "Did you grab the lids and the jars?"

Both Bar and Lizzy laughed. After he smacked himself on the forehead, they climbed back up the ladder to retrieve the forgotten boxes.

Chapter 20

January 1929

Months had passed, and Frank and the Goomahs had not found Lizzy. Obsessed, he thought about her every day. When he felt angry, he swore he would put her in concrete boots and drop her in Lake Michigan if she showed up or he found her. His obsession grew to rage when he imagined her with someone else. "That just won't do," he mumbled. Frank's imagination didn't lie. Over those months, Lizzy grew to find Bar's love made him a worthy courtier.

In January, a woman no one in town knew anything about checked into the Boulton Inn. She walked around the village without a gentleman's escort. She ducked into shops and opened any unlocked doors to buildings, in Boulton, which included most doors. Her actions created talk among the locals.

When she had a drink and dinner at the Boulton Inn, she commented about the excellent moonshine to the barkeep. She asked, "How did you come by this?"

The man smiled and said, "It's a local concoction made by two men, Moonshine Moore and Bar." The bartender started to explain Bar's nickname, but the woman interrupted and said, "Where can I buy a jug? I want to take it back to Chicago."

"I can sell you a jug right now."

She laughed and said, "Well, I will be tempted to drink it before going back to Chicago, but I'll take one. Al Capone will love to know about such a great moonshine. Please give me a jug and put it on my tab."

Al Capone's name rang bells with anyone in Boulton when Mae visited the town. For most, he still had a Robin Hood image. Picking up his drink from the bar, a man walked over to the woman and stood by her table.

"Did you say you know Al Capone?"

"Indeed."

"What brings you to our little neighborhood?"

The woman gestured toward the chair across the table, and the man took a seat.

"We've not been introduced. She reached out a gloved hand and said, "I'm Mae Capone."

The man stood and bowed, "I'm Ben Lehe. Nice to meet you, Mrs. Capone." As he retook his seat and repeated, "What brings you to our neighborhood?"

Of course, Mae didn't tell the truth. She didn't tell him about her friendship with Frank. She didn't tell him she felt sorry for Frank, who had not stopped pining about Lizzy's loss. Al didn't want her to go but felt if anyone could find Lizzy, it would be Mae. His concern for Lizzy forced her hand to visit one more town the Goomahs had not searched. Al wanted to put the Lizzy business behind them so Frank would be more focused on his work. He told Mae, "Go if you must, but be very careful."

Instead of telling Ben the truth, Mae told a lie. "I'm here looking for investment possibilities." Mae's words were music to Ben's ears. He said, "I am the mayor of this town, and," as he narrowed his eyes and made a sweeping gesture with a hand in the air, "I can tell you all you want to know about Boulton. So that's why you searched the town all over today."

"Well, before I talk to anyone, I like to look around."

"Why Boulton?"

"A good friend of mine, Lizzy Lee..."

The man looked shocked and said, "THE Lizzy Lee?"

"Oh, you've heard of her."

"I've actually had the pleasure of attending a play she stared in at Chicago's Auditorium Theater a few years back."

"Lucky you. Anyway, Lizzy told me about this town."

Ben said, "Well, what do you know? I didn't know she had a connection here."

While they talked, the barkeep stood behind the bar and as close as he could to listen to their conversation. The barkeep had a very close working relationship with Bar. He also happened to know Lizzy lived with him. He and the Hoffmans included everyone who knew about the relationship. At the same time, the barkeep's knowledge of Al Capone differed from Ben's, so he kept quiet and listened.

Mae continued, "Well, as you may know, my husband has a lot of money." She repeated two words, "A lot. So, I'm looking to see if Boulton is an investment opportunity."

Ben perked up.

Mae drew him in. "By the way, I haven't seen Lizzy in a while. You know what she looks like. Have you seen her recently?"

The barkeep held his breath and hoped Ben knew nothing of Lizzy.

"It's crazy," Ben said, "I'm the mayor, and I had no idea Lizzy Lee had a connection here."

The barkeep took a deep breath and thought, 'It's because you are clueless, my old friend.'

Lizzy thought Frank had given up the search, so she began to wander into Boulton because of cabin fever. She walked around Boulton the second day after Mae Capone arrived. When Mae inspected clothing and materials at the town's only dress shop, she could not believe what she saw outside the window. Lizzy walked past her. Startled, Mae considered her options. First, she hoped Lizzy didn't come into the dress shop because Mae wanted to remain incognito to Lizzy. She released a sigh of relief when Lizzy walked across the street. By her long absence from Frank, Mae figured Lizzy would run and hide if she saw Mae. She was correct in the assumption. Quickly, she asked the store owner if she knew the woman walking across the street.

"Not really. Never seen her before today."

Mae nodded and said, "She looks like someone I once knew."

"Maybe you should go out and introduce yourself or re-introduce yourself," the owner said.

With one hand on her face, Mae said, "No, I would be embarrassed if she wasn't who I thought she was." The shop owner fell for the ruse, and Mae continued. "Maybe you know where she is staying."

"As I said, I don't know, but maybe Berta Hoffman knows. She came in a few months ago and bought clothes for a young woman who showed up on their farm. It's the strangest thing, how the Hoffman's take in strangers."

"Hoffman? The name doesn't ring a bell with me." Mae waved a hand to end the conversation, "Oh well. I guess I was only hoping to see an old friend." Mae returned to looking at the clothing as if she had given up knowing the stranger. In reality, she thought, 'These country bumkins sure have a poor taste in clothing.'

Chapter 21

Late January 1929

The next morning, Mae packed her bags, had the Innkeeper carry them, and put them in her car. When Mae stepped outside, Ben greeted her. The two had arranged a visit so the mayor could show her around the town. The night before, he had said, "Let me give you a guided tour." In her excitement of finding Lizzy, Mae had forgotten. The mayor looked surprised that her bags sat in the trunk of her car.

Mae genuinely reached out and gently grabbed one of his hands and said, "I'm sorry, Ben. Something came up in Chicago, and I must return home."

"You don't have time for the tour?"

"It is really urgent. I'm going to have to take a rain check."

"Is there anything I can help you with?"

Mae looked into his eyes. The mayor could see why Al loved the beautiful young lady. "I'll give you a ring when I return." She waved goodbye as she walked to her car.

When Mae sat in the car, she looked around to make sure Lizzy was not in the town where she could see her. Mae knew she couldn't seek out Lizzy because she would run from her. She put the car in gear and drove two hours back to Chicago.

In Chicago, Mae didn't seek Al first but hurried to find Frank. He was in a meeting, but Frank froze when Mae stuck her head in the door. Mae nodded her head back as if to say, 'Come see me.' Frank pointed to one of the others and said, "Take over." He promptly walked out the door and followed Mae down a hallway. She turned into an open room, smiled at Frank as he followed her into the room, and closed the door.

Frank's mind spun; he already knew Mae had news that would make him happy and sad at the same time. Mae reached out, put her

155

arms on Frank's shoulders, and said, "I found her!" She wanted to scream it but kept stoic. Frank froze. Although he anticipated this moment, he didn't anticipate how he would feel. Anxiety overwhelmed him. He was surprised by the overwhelming desire to love Lizzy mixed with the thought of killing her. Mae allowed him a moment to reflect on the news and then said, "She is in a small town called Boulton. I didn't let her see me. I only know a farm family may know where she stays. A family by the name of Hoffman should know. The mother, Berta, should know."

Frank clenched a fist in a moment of triumph. He would have kissed Mae but realized if Al saw him, he would be dead. He walked back to the meeting and told the group to carry on. He had business to attend to in Indiana. He motioned for the Caddy driver to follow him. An hour later, Frank was in Hobart, where he met two of his gunmen. He instructed them to go to Boulton, find the Hoffman farm, and retrieve Lizzy.

Two days later, John walked to the back of his house to make sure the well-pump had not frozen. It was a daily chore when the temperatures were so low. He stopped and stood still. He saw a set of tracks in the snow leading up to the kitchen window. John examined the footprints and knew no one in the Hoffman family made those tracks. He was stunned someone had looked into their kitchen window without his knowledge. 'A peeping tom in the middle of winter. It makes no sense,' he thought. He had no idea it was someone from the Northwest Outfit. He looked out across the snowy field and saw the tracks led to a wooded area south of the house. He assumed it was where they had parked their car.

John informed the family. "Someone has been spying on us," he said after he had gathered the family. He stared at the floor. "Nothing like this has ever happened. What does it mean?"

Fritz spoke up first. "It's Frank's goons looking for Lizzy." John studied Fritz for a moment, who continued, "Everyone in Boulton knows we took in a lost young woman. If Frank's still searching for her, somehow, he found out we helped her. I'm pretty sure no one knows she's now with Bar. He keeps things pretty secret. We will be Frank's target."

"Damn," Karl mumbled. "It has begun."

John said, "Well, they must have come just after sunset or before sunrise. There's no reason they would have snuck up to the house when the lanterns are off in the middle of the night. There's nothing to see." John tapped on the table. He had an odd sense because he could smell blood. He felt it was some sort of omen, and it brought a notion of fear. In reality, there was a simple explanation for John smelling blood. The winter air had thinned the mucus in his nostrils. John had no idea that caused him to smell blood – his own. But the smell motivated his army training, and he took the lead for the Hoffman family defense.

Looking around the table where the family sat, he said, "Here's what we will do. We will set up a watch from the barn." He pointed at Fritz, "You will take the first three hours to watch after sunset. I will take the first three hours before sunrise." Karl, you check in on us to make sure we are okay."

The brothers nodded. The younger boys heard the scariest news they had ever heard, yet Patrick didn't feel fear. He knew his father and older brothers would protect the place, and they would be alright. While John busied himself making plans, Patrick and Samuel began to play with their toy soldiers.

John looked at Berta and said, "You had better start to make plans to go to your cousin's place in Indianapolis."

She looked at John and calmly but firmly said, "I'm not leaving you here alone. This is our home. I know you will protect it and us." Proud of what she had said, John pursed his lips and reached out and put a hand on Berta's hand. It was then John heard Patrick making gunfire sounds in the other room.

Darkness came at five p.m., so Fritz ate an early supper, went to the barn, and crawled up into the loft. He assembled a make-shift, straw bench to watch through a window. He took no lantern with him because it would give him away. Even though he shivered in the chill of the night, he stayed next to the window. An hour and a half into the watch, Karl joined him and brought cookies Amelia had baked and hot chocolate Berta had warmed on the stove. The bundle of chocolate cookies Karl handed Fritz warmed his fingers.

Karl smiled and said, "You can't catch the bad guys without cookies." The moon poured light into the window where he could see Fritz's smile. They could also clearly see the house and the surrounding field, but no one approached by eight p.m. John doused the lanterns and candle, so all the lights were off. The boys gave up the watch, walked to the house, crunching snow as they walked, and proceeded to the warmth of their beds.

The next morning, at five a.m. John rose, dressed, and then made coffee. He sat in the dark to drink it. Both Karl and Fritz tiptoed into the kitchen. Fritz found the coffee kettle in the dark and poured a glass each for him and Karl. They sat with John in the darkness.

"What are you two both doing up?" John asked.

"We are not letting you go out alone," Fritz said. "I have a hunch." John always trusted Fritz's hunches. He was like his mother, Berta, with insight into uncanny situations. They finished the coffee, grabbed their guns, and headed for the barn. They didn't know Berta stood at an upstairs window with a heart full of pride and fear. She touched the window, which placed her fingers over John's image, and quietly spoke,

"Good luck, my love." Then, she lit a candle, found her way to the kitchen, and lit it as bright as possible.

The trio took turns looking out of the barn loft window. After two hours, the sky grew from black to dark gray. Amelia cooked a typical breakfast when two men approached the Hoffman home. They had parked in the wooded lot south of the house and snuck up to the house on foot. They both carried rifles. John loosened the window and quietly pointed his rifle out of it. He followed the men across the field. He wondered if his army training remained intact and, if needed, his aim stayed true.

Berta and Amelia busied themselves in the kitchen. Berta made a list of items they needed whenever they returned to town, and Amelia finished preparing a hot breakfast for the men. The two boys stood by John's straw bench and stared at the strangers as they advanced. Soon, the two strangers stood outside the kitchen window and stared in, hoping to see Lizzy. One of the men was fascinated with her said, "I hope Lizzy is in the buff."

The other man turned and looked him in the eyes and said, "Pervert."

When Berta crossed the room to fill a pan with water, one of the men focused on Berta and raised his gun.

"It looks as if the action time has come," John whispered to the boys. He closed one eye and focused on the man pointing his gun toward Berta. John stared down the barrel of the rifle. He wasn't stupid; he knew the men wouldn't do anything until they saw Lizzy, which they wouldn't. But he was wary of the men looking in on Berta. With a smooth pull on the trigger, John watched as the man fell to the ground. He saw the fallen man reach for his shoulder, and John knew he had busted it. With perfect aim, he took the man out of the ability to fire a gun. Both men searched, one standing by the window and the other laying on the ground, but neither could tell the shooter's location. John took one more shot and purposely missed because he intended it to be a warning shot. The bullet skimmed in the snow next to the other man. The men still couldn't tell who was shooting and the person's location. Looking around, the man withdrew his gaze from the house window and reached down to help the wounded man to his feet. Fritz pointed his rifle out the window and prepared to fire. John gently put a hand on the rifle to block Fritz's view. Fritz looked questioningly at his dad, who said, "I've done enough damage. We will see what happens now."

The two men hobbled back across the field and to their car. They left a trail of blood as they escaped. The Hoffman men watched them drive away and turn north at the road. John assumed they headed back to northern Indiana.

Berta put a hand to her heart when the men walked in. "I heard two shots. Were they yours? I've been so worried."

The men sat at the breakfast table and warmed their hands on a cup of coffee Amelia poured for each of them.

John said, "They were mine." He pointed at the window. "The men stood there and watched you fixing breakfast." Berta felt so violated. "I hit one in the shoulder intentionally not to kill him, but he will lay low for a while."

Fritz unabashedly added, "We checked by the window where they had peered in here. The blood isn't pretty. Hope the snow covers it up tonight or tomorrow night."

Berta thwacked Fritz on the back of the head, "I didn't need to know that." She peered out of the window, it was becoming lighter, but she purposely didn't look down to see the blood.

Chapter 22

Early February

Two mornings after John had shot at the intruders, the phone rang. After Berta answered the phone, she quickly handed it to John. He listened intently for a moment. All he said was, "Someplace public. Let's meet at the train station in Larson." John heard no more. The caller hung up.

With a puzzled and worried look, Berta asked, "Was it, Frank?"

"None other."

"Why are you going to meet him?"

163

"I'll be fine; it's in a public place. He doesn't want me. He wants Lizzy."

John sat back down at the breakfast table and thought about it for a moment. Finally, he looked at Fritz and said, "We need to bring Bar and Lizzy into play. Why don't you go over there and invite them to come here for the afternoon?"

Karl stayed Fritz with the wave of his hand. He picked up the telephone and told the operator he wanted Brian Allen Ryan's residence. Lizzy answered the phone. She and Karl talked, and within minutes, they set up the afternoon meeting. When Karl hung up the phone, John waved his hand at it and said, "Damned technology."

John, Berta, Fritz, Karl, Amelia, Bar, and Lizzy sat around the table in the afternoon. Patrick and Samuel played soldiers in the other room. Patrick sensed the tenseness of the meeting and told Samuel, "Let's shoot the bad guys." John overheard the boys playing and shook his head. He was sorry the situation had come down on the Hoffman family, but he never regretted Lizzy showing up, not because she was beautiful, but because she was a person who needed help. He was sad the ruffians treated her like chattel and thought they controlled her. Lizzy chose to leave them, he thought, 'They should forget about her.'

He said, "I'll go straight to the point." He looked at Lizzy, "Frank wants you back. Do you want to go?"

"If it will protect you and your family, I will."

Berta softly said, "That's not the question. Do you want to go back to Frank?"

Bar held Lizzy's hand resting on the table and said, "It's your choice. We will protect you if you don't want to go back."

With her other hand, Lizzy wiped away tears. Berta's eyes teared too. She picked up a napkin and handed it to Lizzy. Then she grabbed one for herself. Berta could feel Lizzy's painful memories because of the intuit she was.

Finally, Lizzy spoke, "You folks have been so kind to a downtrodden fool like me. I cannot ask any more of you."

John spoke again, "What Bar said is right. Simply tell us if you want to stay or go."

Now sobbing, Lizzy only said, "Stay." She touched Bar's face.

He said, "Then it's decided. John, do they know where Lizzy is staying?"

"Frank still believes she lives with us."

"You have to tell him differently."

John walked over to the stove and poured coffee into his cup. "I think keeping them in the dark is the best bet."

Bar knew he could not argue with John.

As Fritz had predicted, it snowed. John, Karl, and Fritz checked outside the window, and the snow hid the blood. Next, the men drove the thirty miles to Larson to meet Frank. The Dodge pickup rolled over and crunched the snow, which had accumulated the night before. Once in Larson, Karl and Fritz stayed in the pickup at John's command, but they located themselves where they could keep an eye on John. When John stepped out of the pickup, he spied Frank, who stood out in the small gathering at the train station. Most people were farmers who gathered to hear a talk by an Extension economist from Purdue. John thought, 'Interesting timing.' The farmers wore coveralls and heavy tan barn coats. Frank wore a slick black overcoat and a black fedora with a shiny, black band with a small feather. For sure, he caught some glances from people in the gathering who wondered who he was.

John greeted him like he would anyone else. He reached out a hand and shook Frank's hand. John marvelously hid his disdain for Frank. He said, "This is your meeting. Get on with what you have to say."

Inwardly, Frank immediately admired John, but he wouldn't say it. Instead, he said sternly, "You have something I want."

John caught the wording and the impression that Frank talked about Lizzy as if she was a possession. He played dumb, "What would that be?"

"Lizzy Lee."

"Oh, to be honest, we took her in after the disastrous night with you, but she doesn't live with us. Your goons showed up at the wrong house."

"Yeah, that. Look, I don't hold it against you. You shot one of my men on your property while protecting your home. I guess, if you had wanted them both dead, they would be."

John nodded in agreement but said nothing else.

"All I want is the girl."

John wanted to correct him and say 'woman,' but he resisted. He sniffed the fresh cold winter air and took in the warm sun; the irony didn't escape John. The cold of evil and the warmth of kindness. Then he said, "That's where we have a problem. She doesn't want to be your chattel again."

Frank's anger grew. He looked at the crowd gathering at the station. "I don't suppose you will tell me where she moved to."

"No."

"I was afraid you'd say no. There will be consequences."

John rolled his eyes and said, "This conversation is over." He walked away.

Nothing out of the ordinary happened for a week. John somehow knew the next attack would happen during the day. So, he, his sons, and Bar took turns guarding the house. On the day John and Karl took cattle to the market, the Northwest Outfit showed up. Fritz and Bar defended the place, with Bar momentarily in the house to retrieve a thermos of hot coffee. Fritz froze when he saw the four strangers climb out of the black Caddy. They had parked at the end of the drive and walked up through John's Jardin to intimidate the Hoffmans. They all carried Tommy guns and wore long, black coats. They became a juxtaposition with John's beautiful garden. Their strategy, unknown to them, kept Bar unaware as they walked up upon the house. Bar dallied talking to the women inside. Alone and breathing hard, Fritz couldn't make up his mind about what to do first. Hesitation cost him. When he stood and aimed, one of the men fired the Tommy gun. A bullet ripped through Fritz's leg and knocked him to the ground. The men marched to him quickly, and one bashed the butt of his gun against Fritz's skull. Bar emerged from the home carrying his Tommy Gun, which he had previously acquired from a customer instead of payment for his hooch. With his boot on Fritz's chest, the man pointed his gun directly at Fritz's head, who lay passed out on the snow. The other three men pointed their weapons at Bar and said, "It wouldn't be wise to shoot at us. You might get one, but I guarantee you and your friend here will both be dead. We don't want you; we want the girl, Lizzy."

Behind Bar, Berta rushed to the door and saw Fritz, her son, passed out on the ground. Moving to Bar's side, she raised her shotgun and pointed it out the door. Slightly surprised, the gang leader laughed. He looked at his other men and said, "She's something else." He then turned back to Berta and gave her the same lecture he had given to Bar. "It will be all over for you. Where is Lizzy Lee?"

Berta looked at the man with hatred in her eyes. "She's not here. My husband told your boss so."

The man removed the shotgun from Berta's grasp. "I'll take the gun before someone else gets hurt."

Berta looked at Bar and nodded for him to stand down. The leader told the men to search the house. Berta started toward Fritz, but the leader stopped her.

She demanded, "Let me attend to my son."

He released her, and Berta ran out into the cold without a jacket and knelt by Fritz. The man with the shotgun to Fritz's face backed off. Fritz came around and started to jump up, but the pain in his leg shocked him. Dazed, he had forgotten he had been shot.

Berta placed a hand on his chest. Fritz had worn a neckerchief to ward off the cold. Berta removed it from his neck and wrapped it around his leg to slow the bleeding. "Just lay here for a moment. I'm going to grab something to treat your leg."

When she stepped back into the house, the men returned to the leader one by one. The last one said, "She's not here." He had Patrick by the scruff of his neck.

Berta cried out, "No. He's innocent."

"Then maybe you will tell us where Lizzy is?"

At the moment, John and Karl drove the farm truck down the long drive and up to the house. They saw Fritz on the ground, who motioned for them to go into the house.

Once in the house, they pointed their guns at the men. Bar picked up his Tommy gun.

The men held their guns up. The leader said, "There is no need for violence here. We just want to know where Lizzy is."

"With me," Bar said.

The leader raised his eyebrows and said, "Here? Now?"

"Don't think I'm stupid."

For such a young child, Patrick, who was farm brawny, swung his leg back and kicked the man who held him up in the air, in the groin. The man dropped Patrick and his gun. The leader said, "This has gone far enough. We shall depart your company and take the matter up another day." John, Karl, and Bar kept their guns pointed at the men as they retreated. "This is only the beginning. It won't end until we retrieve her for Frank."

Berta motioned for them to leave with a look of disgust. She then gathered what she needed to give Fritz first aid. After she had done so, John helped Fritz into the Dodge and drove him into town to see Doc Baines.

After the doctor patched Fritz's wound, John and Berta brought him back home the same night their house had been invaded. The bullet had not struck any bones but ripped a pretty good hole through the skin and muscle on the side of his leg. Doc Bain stitched the wound. The doctor loaned Fritz crutches until he could acquire his own. John felt pride watching Fritz handle the pain well. The doctor told Fritz he could prescribe morphine, but he didn't recommend it. "I've seen and read in the journals too many people become addicted to it."

"I've read that too in the Chicago City Times," Fritz moaned. "Still, the pain is severe. I guess I have to be stronger."

He handed Fritz a bottle of aspirin. "This may help. You should feel better in a week, but it will take weeks before all of the pain is gone. It's February. You should be walking fine by the time spring farming rolls around."

"Thanks for the advice, doc," he said almost sarcastically.

John asked, "Is he ready to go home?"

"Don't see any reason why not. Keep an eye on the wound to ensure it doesn't become infected." The doctor looked at Berta and said, "I know you can take care of the cleaning." Then he looked Fritz in the eyes and said, "Get plenty of rest and try to keep pressure off the leg."

Chapter 23

February 12

In Chicago, a policeman innocently walked into an alley where the North Side Gang conducted a major drug deal with some prominent businessmen. If he had backed away, they would have let him go. He refused and pulled out his gun. Before the policeman pointed it, one trigger-happy gang member shot him dead. The gang concluded the drug deal and left the policeman lying in the alley.

"Last summer, a young woman showed up at our house after being abused and beaten the night before. She had attended a Chicago Outfit retreat at Miller's Point."

The sheriff didn't hesitate, "She was the property of the Chicago Outfit."

"Sheriff!" Berta scorned. There was no love between Berta and the Sheriff from previous incidents.

Sheriff Bucklyn said, "Well, that's how they treat women. You folks should have told me."

Berta quickly replied, "She was so battered, beaten, and afraid, she simply wanted to hide out."

"Still," said the sheriff. "Now you have a war at home!" The sheriff looked at John, whom he respected because of his service during the big war. "Keep me informed from now on."

John nodded but said nothing more. When John and Berta left, the Sheriff called a friend on the Indiana State Police force located in Lafayette.

When his friend answered the phone, the Sheriff asked, "What can you tell me about the Northwest Indiana Outfit coming into the district?"

"Well, we are aware they have a retreat in the district," the man said at the other end of the telephone.

"Can you be more specific?" Silence met the Sheriff's ears. "Well, have you forgotten how to speak?"

"All I can say is that we are investigating, but we have nothing to go on at this point."

"Well, I may have something for you."

His friend listened while Bucklyn shared the situation at the Hoffman farm. John and Berta had withheld from the Sheriff that John shot one of their men. The couple didn't want to bring the police into the situation any more than they had to. They didn't exactly trust their Sheriff.

When Bucklyn finished telling his friend what he knew, there was another long pause. Finally, the man said, "My friend, you might want to steer clear of the situation, it is much larger, and we don't want to mess up the investigation."

They said goodbye, and as Bucklyn put the phone down, he puzzled over the bigger picture. Normally, his State Police friend would jump at the chance to help him.

At home, John pleaded with Berta to take Amelia, Patrick, and Samuel to visit her cousin.

"I don't want to leave you here. I'll go crazy worrying about you."

Bar walked in the kitchen door with Karl. He overheard Berta's complaint and said, "You don't have to worry about him. I've collected a few loyal customers to help guard the place." He spread out his big hands to indicate the home and the family would be protected.

Then the Hoffmans heard the news about a gang slaughter on their brand-new radio. They gathered around the radio and listened to WLS out of Chicago. When the news came on, the murder of the seven men from the North Side Gang dominated the evening broadcast.

The reporter said, "We have been keeping you up-to-date all day long on a senseless and gang-related shooting at North Clark Street. Details are sketchy, but we believe the attack was staged by the Chicago Outfit and some rogue police officers." The Hoffmans and company became silent and continued listening. "All seven murder victims are said to have been involved in the murder of a policeman two days ago while he walked his morning beat."

John stood up and turned off the radio. "We've heard enough." He turned back to the family and then singled out Berta. He took a knee in front of her and held her hands. "I implore you to retreat to your cousins. You will be safe there."

Berta considered her options after hearing the recent news. She put a hand on John's cheek and looked into his imploring eyes for a moment. Then scribbled a phone number on several pieces of paper. She gave each of them the phone number, pointed at all the men one by one, and said, "It's my cousin's phone number. If anything happens to anyone, call me immediately. I don't want to worry all day long."

Each of the men took one of the pieces of paper. Karl handed one to Fritz, who sat at the end of the table with his leg propped up on another chair.

The following morning, Berta loaded up their car and left for Indianapolis with Patrick, Samuel, and Amelia.

After hiding out for a week, in which Frank paced his home in Hobart, he finally thought enough was enough. Calling a gathering, he said, "I'm done hiding." He gave four men assignments to complete while he was gone. He pointed at three other men and, matter-of-factly, said, "You are coming with me." He rolled an extended hand into the air and told them, "Pack clothes for a few days. We will stay at Miller's Point until we locate the moonshiner."

One of the men was the Caddy driver. Frank ordered him to take him to Miller's Point, and the other two men trailed them in a second car. It was late when they arrived; Frank used the time left to plan for the search.

Frank never understood that the problem began long before the drunken night. Sitting in the winged chair, he smoked a cigar and drank near beer. He ordered the other men to drink only near beer. "Tonight, we will not repeat the drunken scene that caused the problem we now face."

Frank reviewed what they knew. Lizzy had been in Boulton when Mae visited. He assumed she lived out of town because the still in which they made moonshine would require some discretion.

He continued, "Tomorrow, I want you to go to the bar where Mae found the hooch. Order a jug but press for the name of the person who makes it."

Bar and his friends took turns staying at Hoffman's house for the past week. All the men guarded the house in shifts along with the Hoffmans. Lizzy glued herself to Bar. None of them knew how to cook like Berta and Amelia. So, the meals were simple. The menu included eggs and bacon or pancakes and bacon in the morning and in the evening; it consisted of steaks or hamburgers with canned vegetables from the Hoffman cellar. John had become very adept at making lemonade, and they always had coffee on the stove. They didn't drink any alcohol while they waited for the inevitable.

The second morning they gathered for breakfast; Karl cooked the pancakes. Fritz shoveled a forkful of pancake into his mouth, and with that mouthful, he mumbled, "This is kinda burnt."

Karl extended his arm in Fritz's direction and placed his hand on the table. He said, "Remember, we have a rule. If anyone complains, they cook the next meal."

Fritz held up a bite of pancake on his fork and said, "Best damn burnt pancake I've ever had." He smiled toothily at his brother.

Arriving in Indianapolis, Berta hugged her cousin, Clara Ward, and said, "Thank you for taking us in on short notice."

"Don't mention it." Then Clara saw Amelia, whom she recognized from the factory where they had worked together before Amelia joined to Hoffman family. The two hugged tightly. "It's great to see you again. You look radiant given the situation."

Amelia smiled and said, "It's good to see an old friend."

Clara wiped her hands on her sleeves and grabbed Patrick and Samuel gently by their chins. "And look at you two! You are growing so fast." Clara invited them all in. "The place is small, but you'll have the run of it because I work six shifts per week and average ten hours on each shift."

Berta rolled her eyes and asked what they could do.

"You are doing it. You got away from the hoodlums and Capone. By the time Berta visited Clara, everyone had heard about the "Valentine's Day Massacre." Clara then said, "It is a shame what's going on in Chicago." They all stood quietly for a moment. Patrick and Samuel had already excused themselves to the other room. They brought their army men and began to play with them. Clara finally said, "Let me show you around."

The week passed, but the Hoffman's still hadn't seen the Northwest Outfit. John realized he had incorrectly assumed they would be back immediately with reinforcements. Because he didn't have the mind of a criminal, he never considered Capone had ordered all of the Outfit to lay low. At the beginning of the second week, the sheriff drove his car up Hoffman's lane. When John opened the door and let the sheriff in, the man smelled the bacon. Being heavy set, he hoped they'd offer him leftovers, which they did.

Sitting at the table, while Lizzy brought an egg and some bacon, the sheriff said, "I didn't come out here to mooch a second breakfast, but I thank you."

"I assume you have news," John said.

"That I do." The sheriff pulled a toothpick out of his shirt pocket, began to pick at his teeth, and said, "It looks like they are back. Three strange men visited the town. They even visited me. Said, they are looking for Lizzy Lee."

Bar leaned forward with both hands on Lizzy's shoulders.

"I didn't owe them anything, so I told them to get lost." He harrumphed, "Surprisingly, they did so without a fuss. I drove out here in case they came here."

"Not yet, but they will."

Suddenly, Lizzy spoke. "This has gone on long enough. I should give myself up to them."

Bar wrapped his arms around her and exclaimed, "No way!"

The sheriff agreed with Bar, stood, and looked at Lizzy, "We abolished slavery many years ago. These folks here will protect you."

He clicked his tongue, smiled at Lizzy, and said, "Thanks for the bacon and eggs." Then the Sheriff looked at John and said, "How do you have so many beautiful women under one roof."

John simply nodded his head toward the door. The sheriff rolled his eyes, excused himself, and returned to his patrol car.

February 21

Berta sat with Amelia at what they now called their 'hide-away-house.' She said, "If John is still alive, I will kill him. Why hasn't he kept us up to date?"

To calm Berta, Amelia said, "You did say call if anything happened. It means nothing has changed."

"Still, he can be so blockheaded one moment and so caring the next." Berta sobbed a little and then worked to calm herself and hold her feelings inside, which Berta did the best.

Immediately after the sheriff left, the phone rang in the Hoffman home. It was Frank on the other end.

John took the phone from Karl and listened.

Frank said, "Do you know the Oakwood dam?"

John said, "Yes."

Frank said, "We want to get the situation behind us as much as you do. Here's the offer. You bring Lizzy and hand her over, and we leave. Or we engage in a stand-off, and the winner takes all."

A utility company completed the Oakwood Dam in 1925. The earthen part of the dam stood 58 feet above the river and the banks on both sides. After many family trips to watch the power company build the dam, John was very aware of its location. He recalled several oak and cottonwood trees at the base of the dam. He considered the trees would provide some protection in the event of gunfire.

John simply said, "We will be there at seven a.m. tomorrow."

Frank verbally agreed and hung up the phone.

John turned to the eagerly waiting group and explained the conversation. His military training kicked in with the force of his mighty Percheron horses. He firmly added, "Lizzy isn't going."

She protested.

"We are not going to operate that way."

Bar smiled and blurted out, "We will blast them, right?"

John didn't know how to answer Bar's enthusiastic question. He reached a hand out to Bar, "Let's be calm and take it one step at a time. We want the tactical advantage."

Bar settled down and listened to John, who said, "As far as we know, they don't know the location of your place. I don't feel they are trying to draw us out of the house on a ruse. Just the same, Lizzy, we will drop you off at Moonshine's house in the morning. Then we will go meet them."

Lizzy wasn't happy with the command but decided she had another course of action. She would do it on her own if she did anything. She asked John, "You will meet him at seven a.m., right?"

John nodded an affirmative.

"John and his crew will be there a half-hour before."

John nodded and had figured that would be the case.

Lizzy simply said, "You guys take care of yourself." Then she looked at Fritz and said, "I don't know if I can take one more of you being harmed on my account."

Fritz placed two fingers on his forehead and then saluted them toward Lizzy.

Chapter 24

February 22

At six a.m. on the cold February morning, the Hoffmans prepared to meet the Outfit. In all, Bar called together four others to help fight the Outfit. He decided they might be outgunned because the Outfit had more Tommy Guns, but Moonshine's gang presented more people.

Earlier, around five a.m., Bar left Lizzy with Moonshine. She would soon accomplish precisely what she had hoped would happen. She had plans. She began to help Moonshine with the still, but she kept a close eye on the clock. She knew Frank's procedures. He would order the men to go earlier, around six a.m., to set up. Frank always sent people earlier to gain the jump on others. She figured he'd leave to join them by six-thirty. At six o'clock, Lizzy asked Moonshine if she could borrow his Model T for the morning.

He said, "You ain't gonna go to the Oakwood Dam, are you?"

"I will not, but I need to go. Can I borrow it?"

Moonshine gave Lizzy anything she wanted. "It's unlocked. Don't do something stupid, or John will never let me hear the end of it."

Lizzy tossed the towel she had been using on the counter and ran into the house. She quickly changed clothes because she had laid the little black dress out the night before. She donned the black dress she wore when Frank first met her. The dress, she hoped, would serve as a distraction for what she wanted to do. She pulled on long black gloves, opened her purse, and checked to see if the revolver was still there. She strapped it to her inner thigh, put on a heavy coat, and walked out of the house."

She drove straight to Miller's Point, which only took fifteen miles from Moonshine's place. She parked far enough away so Frank would not hear her approach. As luck would have it, the Caddy driver had already left with the other men. She knew or hoped Frank was alone in the retreat house. She snuck into the back door, walking tenderly in the snow in her high heels. She heard Frank milling about upstairs and took a seat at the table where she could see Frank when he came down the stairs. In a twist of thoughts, she had brought a jug of Moonshine's hooch. She grabbed two crystal glasses and a carafe and filled all three with the moonshine. When she stopped pouring, she heard Frank walking down the stairs. Frank froze when he saw her sitting at the table. The irony of his desires, both good and bad, overwhelmed him.

She poured a drink for both of them.

"It's a little early for that, right?" Still, he accepted the glass from her.

"Or maybe it's a lot too late," she said.

They clinked the glasses. Lizzy suggested he have a seat at the other end of the table from her.

Everything Frank wanted — Lizzy — sat at the table. He sat at the other side of the table, not because she told him to, but so he could look her over. "Mighty fine dress, you have. But you are the queen of fashion."

"Why, thank you, Frank."

Lizzy kept her eye on him. She wanted to drink the entire jug with what she was about to do. She said, "Do you even know what went wrong?"

"I suppose you are going to explain it to me." He casually twirled the moonshine in the glass he held.

"If I have to. Hollywood went wrong. I couldn't stand the men in there, and the longer we stayed there, you became more like them. No! You became exactly like them." Lizzy hesitated and took another drink. "I guess you could say Hollywood changed both of us. Then, you bring hell down on a good family and their friends. Your men shot and tried to kill them just because you wanted me back. That's not love. It's lust and greed."

Frank considered his options. Lizzy had dressed to the 'T' and didn't appear to have a gun. He wanted to make love to her and shoot her at the same time.

He said, "Is there any chance for us?"

Lizzy pursed her lips and slowly shook her head. "No."

The gesture helped Frank narrow his options. He reached for the gun holstered to his side, but Lizzy had her non-drinking hand on the pistol between her legs. She winced and shot Frank in the groin. She felt a stinging sensation on her inner thigh when her gun fired. Shocked, Frank couldn't move. Lizzy slowly stood, pointed her pistol at Frank, and shot him in the head. Frank slid off of his chair and onto the carpeted floor.

Taking one last gulp of moonshine, Lizzy grabbed the jug of moonshine so nothing could be traced back to Bar. She turned and walked to Moonshine's Model T, emptying the jug onto the snow as she walked. She took one last look at the house. Her body shook as she felt a massive release from torture. Then drove away.

Chapter 25

February 23

When John and company approached the dam, they saw the Outfit gang had already set up their positions. Wounded Fritz stayed back in the pickup and watched for anyone who might try to sneak up on the Boulton Gang; a moniker Bar had given them that morning. Of course, none of them, including John and his men, knew Frank had died only a few minutes ago. From the Outfit, each of the three men stood next to a large tree if they needed to take cover. He stood on higher ground than the Outfit men with his military training. He posed with his rifle pointed at the men. John knew the Outfit had made a big mistake.

They had positioned themselves with the 58-foot earthen dam behind them. They were trapped between the dam and the Boulton Gang. John stared through furrowed eyes and gritted his teeth like he often did during battles in the war.

The leader of the Outfit expected Frank would come up behind John. It could be the only reason he wasn't with them. He shouted out into the cold with a frosty breath, "Did you bring her?" The cold air stung his lungs.

John tilted his head and said, "What do you think?"

Everyone with John stepped behind a tree. The inevitable shoot-out began. For the Outfit, it stemmed from the frustration of not finding their target. For the Boulton Gang, it primarily stemmed from their rage at these killers invading the peaceful county.

Because of the trees, many shots embedded into the bark and left no one shot. Then the moment came. One of the gangsters had overloaded his Tommy gun magazine with 30 rounds instead of 25. When his gun jammed, he widened his stance to unjam the weapon. John saw the man's lower leg and fired. He could tell it was a direct hit on the bone. The man fell and screamed. Bar had a clear shot and put a bullet into his heart.

The man's blood splattered the once pristine snowy ground. John had a clear sight of Bar. He put a thumb-up and motioned with his hand so Bar could see it. Both understood if they didn't kill these men, their pursuit would not stop. Karl fired but hit only a tree, the other men from the Boulton Gang had about the same effect as Karl, but altogether the firings overwhelmed the Outfit men. For some unknown reason, the remaining two men retreated, but the only choice was to retreat up the dam bank. They occasionally fired back at John, Karl, and the other men as they slowly climbed the earthen part of the dam. They didn't notice Bar quickly running across the frozen river and climbing up the other side of the dam, much quicker than they could on the earthen side. The two gangsters saw thick brush on the far side of the dam. They ran from the earthen portion and onto the concrete part of the dam. They took turns firing back at John and company. When they ran across the concrete dam, they saw they were a few feet from escaping.

They ultimately lost sight of Bar, who stepped out of the thicket and gunned both men down with his Tommy Gun.

John and Frank had a full view of the men after Bar shot them. One fell at the apex of the concrete dam, laid there, and died; the other man fell off the side of the dam and slid all the way down into the river.

"Damn," John murmured, "while the river is frozen, he fell into the part where the waterfall kept a pool of water rushing under the ice. It will be spring before they find him."

Karl smirked, turned, and gave a thumbs-up to Fritz in the pickup. In return, Fritz honked the horn loudly and flashed the headlights. John acknowledged Fritz's celebration with a nod. "The nightmare finally ends for Fritz and all of us." But he then said, "Well, it looks like the real dirty work needs doing now." He and Karl walked back to the pickup, put their guns in the back, and climbed into the cab with Fritz. John took control of the wheel, drove to a bridge to cross the river, and then proceeded to the Oakwood Inn on the other side of the river.

Chapter 26

February 23

John knew the owner of the Oakwood Inn, which was located feet away from the dam. He found him hidden behind the taproom bar when he entered the Inn. The night before, John had warned him, by phone, there would be gunfire. When he found the owner cowering behind the bar, John said, "It's okay. The good guys won. You can come up now. It's over."

The man asked, "Was anyone hurt?"

"The three gangsters are dead," John reported matter-of-factly.

"I meant of your crew."

"Thank God, no." For a moment, John thought about the impact on life if one of the crew had been shot. Then asked, "Can I use your telephone?"

As simple as picking up the phone, listening for the operator, and asking for the sheriff, John fulfilled his duties of letting the authorities know what happened. John asked him to come up to the dam. When he hung up the phone, he held his hand up in the air with two quarters in his fingers and said, "I want to make a long-distance call." He lowered his hand onto the bar with a question mark on his face and left 50 cents. He asked, "Will that be okay?" The owner nodded approval. John waited for the operator and then gave her Clara's number, which he remembered by heart. Clara was at work, so Berta answered the phone, anxious for happy news from John.

There was a moment of silence from John's end of the line because he didn't enjoy talking about emotional news over the telephone. Even with the silence, Berta could hear John breathing. She knew it was him. John listened to a sigh of relief from Berta.

Berta apprehensively said, "Tell me no one was hurt."

"Only the bad guys. It's over." John distinctly heard crying from Berta. John asked, "Are you alright?"

"You know these are tears of joy, John."

Softly he said, "I know. Please come home. We miss you."

In a moment of levity, Berta asked, "Are you sure it isn't Amelia's cooking?"

"I'm partially guilty there. I hope to see you in a few hours. We have a mess to clean up here at the dam, and it may take a while."

He hung up the phone, looked at it, and then mumbled, "I know how to use it, but I don't prefer to do so."

The sheriff arrived with lights flashing and the siren blasting on his patrol car. Following right behind him, the coroner drove up in the county meat wagon.

Stepping out of his car, the sheriff asked, "How many?" "Three," John pointed across the river. "One over on the other side of the river." Then he pointed to the dam. "One on top of the dam, and oh shit," he said, twirling his finger in the air like water going down a drain. "We might not find the other one who slid under the ice until spring." He pointed to the base of the dam.

Looking around, the sheriff saw Karl and Fritz near the pickup and the rest of the crew across the river, but he didn't see Bar. "Where's Bar?"

Bar walked up behind the sheriff and said, "Right here." Without hesitation, Bar turned around and put his hands behind his back. "I shot and killed all three. You might as well, take me in."

The sheriff started to wave him off but said, "I hate to do this, but I suppose I have to until the judge weighs in on the situation."

In the meantime, Lizzy drove back to the Hoffman house, where she found Clara's number and called to talk to Berta. There was no answer, so Lizzy hoped it meant John and the gang were successful, and Berta was on her way home. When she hung up, she scanned the kitchen and saw it was a mess. She immediately decided to clean it up.

At some point, John and Karl returned to the Hoffman home where Lizzy had successfully cleaned up the kitchen and the dishes. Lizzy had been so busy cleaning the kitchen she forgot she still wore the black dress. Although her hair was a mess, she looked quite the site as the men entered the room.

Karl uncharacteristically commented, "Well, we are celebrating the occasion, but I think you are a little overdressed." Lizzy turned beet red when she remembered her attire. She started to go change but realized her clothes were at Bar's place. Karl said, "Relax, you can explain the story later."

A moment later, Fritz hobbled into the kitchen. Happy to see John, Fritz, and Karl safe, Lizzy smiled, but she grew concerned. She reached for the kitchen table to steady herself and slowly sat on the chair. "Where is Bar?" She asked.

Karl chimed in, "Don't worry, he's safe."

Fritz limped to the kitchen table, sat down, and propped his leg up. "He's inspecting the county jail right now."

Lizzy folded her arms on the table and pressed her forehead against them. "Why am I attracted to men who get into trouble?"

John put his hand on her shoulders and said, " All of our actions were self-defense. I expect we will receive a phone call within the hour from the judge, who will tell us we can get him. You and Karl can go. Fritz and I will wait here for the women to return."

Chapter 27

February 1966

In her sixties, Lizzy drove back to Miller's Point once per week to visit someone at the home. The Northwest Outfit had long retreated from the Boulton area. Due to the nonpayment of property taxes, the county acquired the home. The commissioners quickly handed it over to a private party who converted the big home from a gangster retreat into an elderly care home. The home housed 13 men and women ranging from 61 to 93. Even though she visited every week, she still felt trepidation when viewing the place. On the anniversary of shooting

Frank, she recalled the ominous memories of the fatal day. Lizzy stared at the building from the drive before she walked in to visit a loved one.

When she stepped into the parlor, Berta, now 81 years old, sat with a warm smile and looked at her. Lizzy responded with her own smile, ran to Berta, and gave her a big hug. The two women sat beside each other on the sofa. Still feeling odd about where she sat on that day, Lizzy became melancholy for a moment.

"What's wrong, dear?" Berta asked.

"There's something I have not told you."

Berta put a hand on Lizzy's knee and asked, "What is it?"

Lizzy saw Frank's body on the floor in a pool of blood in her mind. The vision was only feet from where they sat. She put her hands to her face and began to sob. Berta sat patiently until Lizzy recovered. Their weekly session never started so sadly. Berta began to feel as if Lizzy had brought bad news and struggled to say anything. Slowly, Lizzy began to speak while waving her hands in front of her face to shake off the melancholy feelings she was experiencing and block the image of Frank on the floor. Then she waved one hand directly at her face to cool herself.

Lizzy blurted out with no more hesitation, "I shot and killed Frank 38 years ago right here." She dabbed her eyes. "I mention it now because today is THAT day. It overwhelmed me, I guess."

The stately older woman patted Lizzy's knee. "It was a long time ago. It was something you had to do." Berta ducked her head and looked into Lizzy's teary eyes. "I do hope you have forgiven yourself."

"I thought I had. Now I fear I have ruined the home for you."

Berta gazed around the room and the house, which had become her home before she would find the grave. She said, "I already knew."

Shocked, Lizzy asked, "How did you know? I only told John, so he knew there was closure on the Frank problem."

Berta took her hand off Lizzy's knee and said, "John and I never held secrets from each other." She sighed, "I do miss that man." She remembered sitting by his hospital bed three years ago as he died in his sleep. "He fought hard, but cancer won him over."

Lizzy put an arm around Berta and said, "Why did you check into this home last year? You know you could have stayed with Bar and me, Karl and Amelia, or Fritz and Kathryn.

"I-I know, but I'd just be in the way."

Lizzy began to protest, but Berta wouldn't have any of it. That was the way of tough ol' Berta.

"Now, girl, you know I'm well off here. The food is great, I read all the books I want from the county library, I watch picture shows in that magical box over there, and I've made several good friends who like to play euchre." Berta hesitated only a moment and asked, "How are the boys?" The families only visited once per month.

"There are all doing very well. Oh! Jonathan returned from the Vietnam War. He's safe and has returned to farming with Fritz. They are making plans to bring him over so he can see his grandma again."

"That's great news. I've missed Jonathan so much."

"How are you and Bar?"

"He's settled into retirement. Who would have thought he'd work 30 years at Delvan Chemicals after retiring from the moonshine business?" She shook her head slightly. "Karl and Patrick keep busy with their families, and, of course, there's the volunteering to coach the youth-group basketball."

"Oh, I'd like to see a game."

Lizzy didn't hesitate, "I'll take you to a home game next week." Lizzy eyed Berta with pride as if she was her daughter." A tear of joy rolled down her face.

"Are you okay?" Berta asked.

"I've never been better!"

While the two women sat silently for a moment, they both reflected on the past in their different ways.

Berta reflected on how Amelia and Lizzy became the daughters she always wanted. She knew Lizzy never forgave herself for endangering the Hoffmans, so she tried to give her some peace of mind. She said, "I'm so glad you came into our lives those many years ago. You sure made life exciting!" She said with a wry smile. "When we reach old age, it is not the accuracy of our memories that's important.

Over time we lose accuracy, but it's more about how we view our memories. The way we view a memory is everything about who we are. Our interaction with memories is so important. You must, must forgive yourself."

Epilogue

Late February 1928

The Outfit found out about the three murdered gangsters in Indiana by virtue of the news. Because Frank's actions were against Capone's commands, he forbid anyone to retaliate in Boulton. It had been a week since the murders. Still, there was no news of Frank. Tired of the Northwest Indiana Outfit bumbling in downstate Indiana, Capone sent his two best men to the retreat to see if Frank held up there.

The men arrived at the retreat two hours later and saw Frank's Cadillac outside the Miller's Point hideaway. Cautiously they stepped up to the front door of the house. As soon as they opened the door, the foul stench of death smacked them in the face. They used handkerchiefs to muzzle themselves and walked into the room with the horrid smell. There they saw Frank lying on the floor.

"Crap," the first man said. "Now, we will have to clean the mess up."

The second man went out the door, puked, and then went to his shed and took out two shovels. The other man rolled Frank up into the carpet and dragged him outside. An hour later, they buried Frank in a remote spot of the woods behind the retreat.

They found the key to the Caddy, and one man drove it home while the other man returned in the car they had driven to Miller's Point. When they met Capone, they told him all of the details. He patted one of the men on the shoulders and said, "You did good." After Capone heard the story from the men, he never mentioned Frank's name again. Frank didn't even become a footnote when historians researched the Chicago Outfit.

-end-

What's next?

Bet and Breakfast

A horror story about staying in someone else's home.

Thanks to https://wallpaperaccess.com/for the artwork.

Made in the USA
Middletown, DE
07 October 2022

12029604R00119